Hulking shapes advanced down the stairs, the shadows closing in. Ronin counted four and knew that there was little hope. Orange light flashed briefly on an upraised sword and Ronin readied himself for the desperate charge up the stairs.

A thin shadow blurred past him, hurled itself like a bolt, leaping obliquely up the stairs, crashing into the now quickly descending figures. The Neer!

There were shrieks, and for a terrible instant, a clawing mass of arms, legs, and torsos were limned in the shuddering illumination of the dying torch, and it seemed as if the bodies hung suspended in the air. Then they all hurtled into the black well of the pit, gaping and irresistible. He tried to catch a glimpse of a face, any face. The Neer's face. But the mass had dropped out of sight and they heard very loud the sickening wet smacks like giant sacks ripped open far Downshaft, reverberating up the ragged sides of the pit.

THE SUNSET WARRIOR

Book One in
*The Sunset
Warrior Cycle*

Eric V. Lustbader

FAWCETT CREST ○ NEW YORK

A Fawcett Crest Book
Published by Ballantine Books

ISBN 0-345-46678-0

Printed in the United States of America

BVG 01

To R.A.L. and M.H.L.
who were there through the best and,
especially, through the worst.

And

To Henry Steig, more than the master artisan.

To survive is not enough.
—Bujun saying

One

ECHOES

RONIN was dying and he did not know it.

He lay quite still and completely naked on the center of an elliptical stone slab which occupied roughly the center of a square, cold chamber. Despite this, tiny beads of sweat glinted in the bristles of his short, black hair. His fine features held no expression whatsoever.

Standing over him, bent, eyes intent, was Stahlig, the Medicine Man. Ronin tried to relax, thinking, This is all a waste of time, as Stahlig's fingers probed and pushed at his chest, moving slowly down toward his ribs on the left side. He tried not to think of it but his muscles had a will of their own and they betrayed him, jumping in pain under the thick fingers.

"Uhm," Stahlig grunted. "Very recent."

Ronin stared at the ceiling; at nothing. What was bothering him? It was merely a fight. *Merely?* His lips curled in distaste. A brawl; rolling in the Corridor like a common—abruptly remembrance blossomed. . . .

His bare arms slick with sweat, his thick sword just

sheathed, heavy at his side, his hands light after almost a full Spell of Combat practice. Walking alone and distracted out of the Hall of Combat into a knot of people, all at once surrounded by loud voices disclaiming hotly, stupidly, and he paid no attention. Something pushed against him and a voice cut through the din.

"And where are you going?" It was cold and affected and belonged to a tall, thin, blond man who wore the obliquely striped chest bands of the Chondrin. Black and gold: Ronin did not recognize the colors. Behind the blond man on either side stood five or six Bladesmen wearing the same colors. Apparently they had stopped a cluster of Students on their way from practice. He could not think why.

"Answer, Student!" the Chondrin commanded. His thin face was very white, dominated by a waxy nose. His high cheeks were pocked and a scar ran down like a tear from the corner of one eye so that it appeared lower than the other one.

Ronin was momentarily amused. He was a Bladesman and therefore practiced with other Bladesmen. But these days he did not have much to do and boredom had led him to practice with the Students also. When he did that, as now, he wore plain clothes and those who did not know him took him for a Student.

"Where I go and what I do is my own affair," Ronin said blandly. "What is your business with these Students?"

The Chondrin goggled at him, stretching his neck forward like a reptile about to strike, and two spots of color appeared high on his cheeks, accentuating the whiteness of the pockmarks.

"Where are your manners, Student?" he said men-

acingly. "Speak with deference to your betters. Now
answer the question."

Ronin's hand strayed to the hilt of his sword but he
said nothing.

"Well," sneered the Chondrin, "it appears this Student is in need of a lesson." As if the words were a
signal, the Bladesmen rushed at Ronin. Too late he
realized that he could not draw his sword rapidly
within the confines of the crowd. Then they were pil-
ing into him, the sheer force of their combined weight
bearing him to the ground, and he thought, I do not
believe this is happening. Instinctively he kicked out as
he was borne under, and had the satisfaction of feeling
his boot smash into flesh that gave way. Almost at the
same moment, a blow along the side of his head
disrupted his enjoyment. Adrenaline spurted and he
punched up and out, and even though he was on his
back and the leverage was not there, he felt his fist
connect as it split open skin, cracked into bone. He
heard a brief wail.

Then the boot caught him in the side and a thick
gauze came down over his brain. He tried to hit again,
could not, struggled with an enormous weight on his
chest. His lungs were on fire and he felt ashamed.
When the boot hit him again, he passed out. . . .

The wave of pain came again but this time he had it
under control and there was only the slightest movement. He looked at the wide head bent over him with
its shaggy brows, rheumy eyes, and creased forehead.

"Ach!" exclaimed the Medicine Man, as much to
himself as to Ronin. "What have you been up to, ah?"
He shook his head and, without looking at Ronin,
turned and put a dark, furry cloth against the mouth of

an opaque white-glass bottle, and turned it upside down. He applied the cloth to Ronin's side. It was cold and the pain subsided.

"So. Dress and come inside." He threw the cloth over the back of a hard chair and disappeared through a doorway. Ronin sat up, his side stiff but now without pain, pulled on his leggings and shirt, then his low leather boots. He stood to strap on his sword, then followed in the wake of Stahlig's body into a warmly lighted cubicle in sharp contrast to the starkly geometrical surgery outside.

Here all was a jumble. Shelves of bound papers and tablets rose like wild ivy from floor to ceiling along three walls. Occasionally gaps appeared in the contents of the shelves, or markers stuck out at odd angles. Stahlig's desk was set close to the far wall, and it was covered completely by mounds of papers and tablets, as were the two small chairs set before the desk. Behind the Medicine Man lay glass cases filled with phials and boxes.

Stahlig did not look up from his work as Ronin entered but he reached out behind him and got a clear bottle of amber wine, and from somewhere produced two metal cups, which he blew into perfunctorily before filling them halfway. He looked up then as he held one out. Ronin took it, and Stahlig sat back and waved an arm expansively.

"Sit," he said.

Ronin had to set his cup down in order to clear away the masses of tablets from the chair. He hesitated with them in his arms.

"Oh, drop them anywhere," said Stahlig with a flick of his thick hand.

Ronin sat and sipped, felt the sweet wine unroll its carpet of warmth along his throat and into his stomach. He took a long swallow.

Stahlig leaned forward, elbows on the masses of tablets, fingers steepled, his thumbs tapping absently at his upper lip. He said: "Tell me what happened."

Ronin, swirling the wine slowly in his cup, said nothing. He sat very straight because of his side.

The Medicine Man dropped his eyes, crumpled a sheet of paper, and threw it into a corner apparently without caring where it landed. "So." He sighed audibly, and when he spoke again his voice had softened perceptibly. "You do not wish to speak of it, yet I know something troubles you." Ronin looked up. "Oh, yes, the old man still sees and feels." He hunched forward over the desk again.

He stared at Ronin. "Tell me, how long do we know each other?" His fingers moved along the desktop. "Since you were very young, since before your sister dis—" He stopped abruptly and color came to his worn cheeks. "I—"

Ronin shook his head. "You will not hurt me if you say it," he said softly. "I am beyond that."

Stahlig said quickly, "Since before her disappearance," as if, even in speech, it was a terrible thing to linger over. "A long time we know each other. Yet you will not speak to me of what troubles you." His hands came together again. "You will leave here and go and talk to Nirren"—his voice had acquired a hard edge—"your friend. Ha! He is a Chondrin, Etrille's Chondrin, and what is his first concern? You are without affiliation—you have no Saardin to order you or protect you. He is without feelings, that one. He pretends friendship, for information. That is after all one of his functions."

Ronin put down his cup. Another time he might have been angry with Stahlig. But, he thought, he truly likes me, watches out for me, he does not realize—yet I must remember that he fears many things, some justly, others not. He is wrong about Nirren.

"No one knows better than I the deviousness of Chondrin," he said. "You know this. If Nirren seeks information from me, he is welcome to it."

"Ach!" Stahlig's fingers flailed the air. "You are not a political animal."

Ronin laughed. "True," he said. "Oh, how very true."

The Medicine Man frowned. "I do not believe you realize the precariousness of the situation. Politics is what rules the Freehold. There has been much friction among the Saardin recently, and it becomes worse daily. There are elements within the Freehold—very powerful elements—who, I believe, want a war."

Ronin shrugged. "I could think of worse things happening." He sipped his wine. "At least the boredom will be relieved."

Stahlig was shocked. "You do not mean that, I know you better. Perhaps you think you will be unaffected."

"Perhaps I will be."

Stahlig shook his head slowly, sadly. "You talk without thinking because there is little for you to do. But you know as well as I that none shall remain unscathed by an internal war. Within this confined space such a foolhardy action can only have disastrous consequences."

"Yet I am uninvolved."

"You are without a Saardin, yes. But you are a Bladesman, and when the time comes you cannot be uninvolved."

There was a small silence. Within it, Ronin took another swallow of wine. He said, finally: "I shall tell you what occurred today."

Stahlig listened to Ronin through half-closed eyes, his blunt thumbs again idly tapping his upper lip. He could have been falling asleep.

"I find it incredible that I should be attacked in such a manner—and by Bladesmen. If I were Downshaft in the Middle Levels—you know the Code as well as I. Fistfights are not for Bladesmen. Any grievances are settled by Combat; it cannot be otherwise. For centuries it has been so. And today I am attacked by Bladesmen led by a Chondrin—as if they were urchins who did not know any better."

Stahlig sat back now. "It is as I have said. Tension, and something more, is in the air. A war is certainly coming, and with it a breakdown of all the traditions that have allowed this Freehold, among all other Freeholds, to survive." He shuddered, just once, a pathetic gesture. "The victors, whoever they may be, will change the Freehold. Nothing will remain the same." He gulped his wine, poured more. "Black and gold, you said. That would be—Dharsit's people. He is one of the relatively new Saardin. A new Order they want; new ideas, new Traditions, so they say. *Their* ideas, I say." He was suddenly vehement, slamming his cup down so hard that the contents flew across his desk, staining the tablets. "It is power they want!" He jumped up in exasperation, flinging the wet tablets away from him, heedless of where they fell.

"Oh, Chill take it! Ask your friend Nirren," he said darkly. "He will know."

"We do not normally talk of politics."

"No, of course not," Stahlig said contemptuously. "He would not divulge the strategies Estrill thinks upon. But I will wager he gathers Corridor gossip from you."

"Perhaps."

"Ah!" Stahlig paused, sitting down once again, and then rushed on as if surprised at having elicited this from Ronin. "As for this incident today, I trust you are not contemplating a precipitous action."

"If by that you mean that you are worried I will use this"—he partially withdrew his blade from its scabbard and slammed it home with a whack—"rest assured I am not interested in being drawn into the world of the Saardin."

The Medicine Man sighed. "Good, because I doubt if Security would believe you."

"What about the Students who witnessed the attack?"

"And jeopardize their chances to be Bladesmen?"

Ronin nodded. "Yes, of course. Well, it is no matter to me. And who knows, sometime I may run into Dharsit's Chondrin at practice." He grinned. "He will have cause to remember me then."

Stahlig laughed then. "I daresay he will."

Boots sounded in the surgery and two figures filled the doorway of the inner cubicle as Ronin and Stahlig turned to look. They did not enter the room. They wore identical gray uniforms with three daggers held in scabbards attached to black leather straps buckled obliquely across their chests: Security daggam. Both had short, dark hair and even features; faces one would never look at twice, faces one would have to study closely to remember.

"Stahlig," said one. He had a crisp, clear voice.

"Yes?"

"Your presence is required. Please pack your healing bag and come with us." He handed Stahlig a folded sheet. The other one did absolutely nothing except watch them. Both his hands were free. Stahlig read the sheet.

"Freidal himself," he murmured. "Most impressive." He looked up. "Of course I shall come, but you must tell me something of the nature of the summons. I must know what to bring."

"Bring everything." The daggam eyed Ronin suspiciously.

"That is quite impossible," said Stahlig impatiently.

"I am his assistant. You may speak freely in front of me," said Ronin. The daggam's eyes swung darkly upon him, then back to Stahlig.

The Medicine Man nodded. "Yes, he is helping me."

"A Magic Man," the daggam said slowly, reluctantly, "has gone mad. We have been forced to restrain him—for his own safety as well as the safety of others. He had already wantonly attacked his Teck. But his health seems to be failing, and—"

Stahlig was already busy cramming phials and paraphernalia into a worn leather bag. Seeing this, the daggam stopped, and instead of finishing his thought he stared stonily at Ronin.

"You are no assistant," he said icily. "You carry a sword. You are a Bladesman. Explain."

Stahlig ceased to fill his bag but remained with his back to them. That does not help, Ronin thought.

"Yes, of course I am a Bladesman, but as you can see I am unaffiliated and so have much free time. So I help the Medicine Man from time to time."

Stahlig finished filling his bag. He turned. "All set," he said. "Lead the way." He looked at Ronin. "You had better accompany me."

Ronin stared at the daggam. "It would certainly relieve the boredom."

The Corridor swept away from them in a smooth, gently curving arc. The walls were painted a gray that at one time had been uniform; now, through years of wear and neglect, there were patches made oily and dark by dirt, areas crusty with grime, sections bleached almost white. Here and there spiderweb cracks extended their fingers like tenacious plants seeking sunlight.

Doorways marched by them on either side at regular intervals. Those with doors were invariably shut. Occasionally an open doorway revealed cubicles dark and musty, debris piled in corners, refuse strewn about the floor. But, beyond the evidence of human detritus, they were empty save for the brief flash of small scurrying bodies: click-click of claw, whip of tail.

Gradually the gray of the walls gave way to a tired lusterless blue. The daggam turned left into a dark passageway in the interior wall of the Corridor and the pair behind them followed. None of them gave a second look at the stalled Lift across the Corridor.

They were on a landing of the Stairwell that ran

vertically along the rim of the core of the Freehold. One of the daggam, the one who talked, reached up into a niche in the wall and removed a torch of tarred reeds bound tightly with cord. He held it in front of him while the other daggam produced flint and a tinder box, got a flame going, and touched it to the torch. It flared and crackled as it caught. Sparks jumped in the air and fell blackly at their feet.

Without a backward glance, the daggam proceeded down the concrete steps. Ronin was surprised to find that they were descending rather than ascending. The little he knew of the mysterious Magic Men indicated that they held a lofty position in the hierarchy of the Freehold. Their talents and wisdom were constantly courted by the Saardin despite their traditional vow to forever work toward the good of the entire Freehold. But it was possible that they were not immune to politicization. By all rights the Magic Man should be quartered on one of the Freehold's Upper Levels, yet they were descending. Ronin shrugged mentally. No one knew much about them except that they were rumored to be strange individuals. If one chose to reside on the fringes of the Middle Levels with the Neers it was no concern of his.

Between each Level the Stairwell doubled back on itself at a landing. They traversed the Levels silently, the shivering torchlight distorting their shadows into grotesque parodies of human shapes, shambling things that danced along the walls and low ceilings, expressionless, unthinking, desireless, receding from and approaching their human counterparts disconcertingly.

At length they reached the proper Level and emerged into a Corridor identical to the one they had quit above, save that here the walls were painted a drab green. They waited while the daggam snuffed the torch and placed it in the niche in this landing.

There was more activity on this Level. Men and women passed them going in either direction and the low hum of distant conversations filled the air like a tidal wash. Perhaps two hundred meters from where they emerged, they came upon a door painted dark green. All the others they had seen on this Level were the same color as the walls. Before the door stood two daggam.

A brief, muffled exchange passed between the four daggam. The shorter of the pair guarding the door nodded curtly, turned, and rapped a peculiar pattern on the door. It was opened by another daggam, and the messengers and Stahlig stepped through. Ronin moved to join them but was stopped short by the palm of one of the guards pressed against his chest. The daggam's jaw jutted. "Where you goin'?" His voice managed to sound bored and contemptuous at the same time.

"I am with the Medicine Man." Ronin met his eyes with a steady gaze. He saw a round, jowly face too large for the small, fat nose and close-set eyes the color of mud. But, thought Ronin, an efficient machine that will respond instantly and unfailingly to orders. I have seen so many.

The square mouth with its thick red lips opened like a reluctant gate. "Don't know anything 'bout it. Move along 'fore you get into trouble."

Ronin felt the pressure from the other's hand and stood his ground. Surprise showed briefly in the daggam's eyes: he was used to a certain response to the application of his power. He recognized fear in others easily, loved creating it, seeing it burn before him as if it were a sacrifice. He saw no fear now, and this disturbed him. Anger flared within him, and his fingers plucked at the top dagger strapped across his chest.

Ronin's hand was on the hilt of his sword when a face appeared from around the still partially open door. "Stahlig, you absentminded—"

The Medicine Man's eyes widened. "Ronin. Wondered where you were. Come along in."

Ronin stepped forward but the daggam still barred his way. The daggam, anger still beating within him, shook his head, and the blade of the dagger gleamed in the Corridor's light.

At that moment Ronin saw another face appear. Long and lean with a cleft jaw filled with determination, a very high, narrow forehead topped by coal-black hair so slick and shiny it had blue highlights, it was dominated by wide-apart eyes of a clear piercing blue, whose penetrating gaze appeared to take in everything while giving away nothing.

"*Qieto*, Marsch. Let the fellow through." The voice was deep and commanding.

Marsch heard the words and automatically moved aside, but the anger refused to die, beating ineffectually at the cage of his burly chest. He glared in silent resentment as the figure moved past him, careful that his Saardin should not see, and thus punish him.

Ronin found himself in an antechamber off which he saw two rooms set at angles. The one on his left was furnished starkly and functionally with a large work table and smallish writing desk along one wall, and a narrow bed along the opposite wall. The room was dark but he could make out a figure sprawled on the bed. Battered and scarred cabinets lined the upper areas of three walls. A lone chair squatted empty in the middle of the cubicle.

The room to the right was less utilitarian. Two walls were lined with low couches and cushioned chairs. The daggam, including the two who had been sent for Stahlig, sat on the couch farthest from the door, amid a meal. In the anteroom two more daggam stood flanking Stahlig and the man who commanded the daggam. Ronin thought they must have torn down some walls in order to make these quarters. Two-cubicle quarters were rare enough Upshaft, but Down here—

"Ah, Ronin," said the Medicine Man. "This is Freidal, Saardin of Security for the Freehold."

Freidal inclined his long body from the waist in a gesture that was somehow theatrical. He did not smile, and his eyes were blank beacons that studied Ronin for another brief moment before he returned his gaze to Stahlig. They resumed their discussion.

Freidal was dressed all in deep gray save for the knee-high boots of the Saardin and the oblique chest stripes of the Chondrin, both of which were silver. Ronin wondered at this: overlord and tactician, eyes and ears, all rolled into one.

"Nevertheless," he was saying now, "do you take responsibility for this man being here?"

"Ach!" Stahlig rubbed his forehead. "Do you think he will walk out with Borros? Nonsense."

Freidal eyed the Medicine Man coldly. "Sir, there is much here that is of the gravest import to the Freehold." The brass hilts of his daggers winked in the light as he shifted easily. "I cannot take unnecessary risks." He spoke in a curiously formal, almost anachronistic manner. He stood very straight and he was very tall.

"I assure you there is nothing to fear from Ronin's presence," Stahlig said. "He is merely observing my techniques, and is here only because I invited him."

"I trust you are not so foolish as to lie to me. That would lead to dire consequences both for you and your friend." He glanced briefly at Ronin and the light turned his left eye into a silver dazzle. Ronin started slightly as the Saardin turned back to Stahlig. A reflection, he thought. But it cannot be, not a flash as bright as that. Then he had it, and now, because he was looking for it, he saw that Freidal's left eye did not move in its socket.

Stahlig put up his hands. "Please, Saardin, you have misunderstood me. I merely thought to reassure—"

"Medicine Man, permit me to make clear my position. I did not wish to summon you. Your presence here disturbs me. Your friend's presence here disturbs me. I am thrust deeply into the midst of a highly volatile Security matter with grave ramifications. Had I my way, no one but my hand-picked daggam would have access to these quarters. However, I am now resigned to the fact that such a course is no longer possible. Borros, the Magic Man, is seriously ill, so my Med advisers tell me. They can no longer help him. They say it is beyond them. Hence, a Medicine Man must be summoned if Borros is to live. I wish him to live. Yet I have little patience with your kind. Please attend him as quickly as possible and leave."

Stahlig inclined his head slightly, an acknowledgment of Freidal's authority. "As you wish," he said softly. "However, may I ask you to recount the events immediately prior to Borros's illness?" Ronin bristled inwardly at the Medicine Man's obsequious tone.

"May I ask what for, sir?"

Stahlig sighed and Ronin observed the lines of tiredness in his face. "Saardin, I would not ask you to defend the Freehold with one arm bound to your side. I ask only that you give me the same courtesy."

"It is essential, then?"

"The more information I have, the greater the chance of helping the patient."

"All right." The Saardin beckoned and a daggam appeared. He had been standing just inside the threshold to the room on the right and they had not noticed him before. A writing tablet lay along the inside of his forearm. In his other hand was a quill with which he drew symbols on the tablet. "My scribe is never far from me," said the Saardin. "He takes down all that I say, and all that is said to me. In this way there can be no—misunderstanding at a later time." He looked from the Medicine Man to Ronin and back again with a neutral gaze. It was impossible to guess what he was thinking. "He shall read from the report made to me earlier today."

"That will be fine," said Stahlig. "But let us go in first, so that I may see Borros's condition."

Freidal bowed stiffly and they moved silently into the shadowy cubicle and over to the cot on which the figure lay. "I apologize for the lack of light," Freidal said without a trace of regret. "The Overheads have recently failed, hence the lamps." Two of the familiar clay pots sat on the work table across from the bed, their flames illuminating the room with an uncertain smoky glow.

The figure lay lashed to the bed—an otherwise unremarkable affair consisting of a wooden frame and large, soft pillows—with leather straps around chest and ankles. Both Ronin and Stahlig leaned closer to get a better look in the low light.

In all ways he appeared singular. He was long-waisted with a thick barrel chest and peculiarly narrow hips. His hands had long delicate fingers tipped with protracted, translucent nails. However, most unusual of all was his face. The head, an elongated oval, was entirely without hair, and the skin, drawn tightly over the scalp and high cheekbones, was of a most peculiarly somber hue with a yellow tinge. His eyes were closed and his breathing was shallow. Stahlig bent at once to examine him.

At that moment the scribe began to recite: "'Recorded on the twenty-seventh Cycle of Sajjit—'"

Freidal raised a hand. "Just the text, if you please."

The scribe inclined his head. "Statement of Mastaad, Teck to Borros, Magic Man. We had been working for many Cycles on the final phases of a Project, the goal of which Borros steadfastly refused to confide in me. I did the mixing and controlling of elements, that is all. For several Cycles Borros had been working nonstop. I would leave him at the end of the sixth Spell and when I returned at second Spell, he would be as I had left him, hunching over his table. Three Cycles ago I arrived to find him immensely agitated. But he would tell me nothing, though I begged him for the sake of his health to—"

"What are these, Saardin?" Stahlig interrupted.

Throughout the scribe's recitation, he had been hard at work probing and listening, trying to ascertain the seriousness of the Magic Man's condition. So he had missed them at first. But he had seen them at last and now he pointed. Ronin bent and saw three small spots, like dark smudges of charcoal, forming a triangle, imprinted on each temple of the hairless head.

Freidal too was looking at the spots, and for the first time Ronin felt a heavy tension fill the room. The Saardin continued to stare at the recumbent body. "You are the Medicine Man, sir," he said carefully. "You tell me."

Stahlig seemed about to answer, then apparently thought better of it. In the silence, Freidal, looking satisfied, lifted his hand again.

The scribe's voice once more took over: "'—let me help him more fully. He refused, becoming abusive. I withdrew. The next Cycle his agitation had increased. His hands trembled, his voice cracked, and on more than one occasion he found cause to insult me. Second Spell this Cycle, when I arrived, he screamed at me to leave. He said he no longer required a Teck. He began to rant incoherently. I feared for his health. I tried to calm him. He flew into a rage and assaulted me, throwing me into the Corridor. I came directly here to—'"

The Saardin made a brief sign and the scribe was silent. Stahlig stood up and turned to Freidal. "Why has this man been restrained?"

The Saardin's good eye blazed. "Sir, I wish to know if Borros will live and, if so, whether his faculties have been impaired. When I have the answers to these questions I shall entertain your queries."

Stahlig wiped the back of a hand across his perspiring brow. "He will live, Saardin. That is, I believe he will. As to his faculties, I cannot tell you until he has regained consciousness and I have had a chance to test his reflexes."

The Saardin thought about this for a moment. "Sir, this man was quite violent when my daggam arrived. He fought them although they wished him no harm. They were forced to subdue him and to make certain he would stay that way. It was as much for his protection as for others'." For the first time Freidal smiled, giving his face the look of a predatory animal. It flashed and was gone, leaving no trace that it had ever been there at all.

Stahlig said: "It is an inhuman way to treat anyone."

Freidal shrugged. "It is necessary."

He left them abruptly, posting two daggam at the threshold to the room and admonishing them to leave as soon as the Medicine Man had satisfied himself as to Borros's condition. "If he dies, I hold you personally accountable," he told Stahlig, and this served as his farewell.

Stahlig hissed softly when they were alone in the room with Borros, the nervous sound of released tension. He sank into the cubicle's lone chair and his shoulders slumped. He clasped his hands in front of him. They trembled slightly. Ronin thought that he looked very frail and very old and he felt pity stir inside him.

"I am a fool." Fatigue. "I should never have asked you to come here. I thought for a moment as I thought many years ago, when I was young and foolhardy. I am an old man and I should know better."

Ronin put a hand on his shoulder. He wanted to say something but no words came to him. Stahlig looked up into his face. "He has marked you now, do not forget that." Ronin tried to smile, found he could not. Stahlig rose then, and returned to his ministration of the Magic Man, turning his back on Ronin, who stood, immobile and silent, regarding the dark countenance of the singular man with yellow skin, strapped to the bed, smoky orange light flickering now and again along the considerable lengths of his translucent fingernails, like the traces of some unimaginably mysterious animal.

So it was that when Borros opened his eyes Ronin saw it first, and he called softly to Stahlig, who was at that moment searching his bag.

The eyes were long, that was all he could tell, for they were in deep shadow and Stahlig was bent over him. "Ah," the mouth said. "Ah." He blinked slowly several times. His eyelids drooped. His lips were dry.

Stahlig lifted a lid, peered at the eye. "Drugged," he said very softly.

"Ah," the Magic Man said.

Ronin leaned over so that they could talk without fear of being overheard. "Why drug him like that?"

"The Saardin would tell us it was to calm him. But I do not believe that was the reason."

"Why not?"

"Wrong drug, first of all. Borros is semiconscious, but he is still affected by whatever it was they gave him. Had he been sedated, he would either be out completely or awake and wondering what had happened to him."

"Ah. Ah."

Stahlig said quite clearly: "Borros, can you hear me?"

The lips ceased their noises and a tension came over the figure. "No," the lips said very weakly. "No, no, no, no—" A bubble of spittle had collected at one corner of the mouth, and now it inflated and deflated with the piteous cry. "No, no."

"By the Frost," breathed Ronin.

The head moved from side to side as the mouth worked. Tendons stood out along his neck and he strained against his bonds. Stahlig reached into his bag and administered something to Borros. Almost at once he quieted. His eyes closed and his breathing became less labored. Stahlig wiped his sweating brow. Ronin began to say something but the old man stopped him with a hand on his arm.

"Well, I have done all I can now," he said in a normal tone. He picked up his bag and they left the room. At the door, he left a message for Freidal with one of the daggam. "Tell your Saardin that I shall return during the seventh Spell to check the condition of the patient."

"What did you find out?"

The homey clutter was somehow comforting. The dim Overheads threw a dismal light. The clay lamps were in a corner, resting precariously on a pile of tablets, waiting to be used. The crumpled paper lay where it had been tossed. Across the room, the darkness of the surgery filled the open doorway.

Stahlig shook his head. "I do not wish to involve you further. It is enough that you have encountered the Saardin of Security."

"But I was the one—"

"I gave the assent." He was angry at himself. "Believe me when I tell you that I am going to forget what I have seen. Borros is just another patient in need of treatment."

"But he is not just another patient," said Ronin. "Why will you not tell me what you have learned about him?"

"It is far too dangerous—"

"Chill take that!" Ronin exclaimed. "I am not a child who needs protection."

"I did not mean—"

"Did you not, then?"

In the small silence that built itself around the two, Ronin recognized a potential danger. If one of them did not speak soon, they would be irrevocably separated. He did not understand why this was and it bothered him.

Stahlig lowered his eyes and said softly: "I—have always thought of you in a certain way. As Medicine Man, many things in life—things that at one time I perhaps wanted for myself—were not allowed me. Both you and—your sister—were very close to me when you were young. And then—there was only you." He said it in a halting, protracted manner, and it was obvious that it was difficult for him. Yet Ronin could not find it in himself to make it any easier. Or perhaps this was not possible. "But I understand that you are a Bladesman now. I know what that means. But every once in a while I remember—that child."

He turned and poured himself a drink, swallowed it at once, poured another and one for Ronin, handing him the cup. "And now," he said, as if nothing had happened, "if you insist, I shall tell you what I have learned."

Stahlig told him that from what he had observed he was sure that Security had had Borros for more than a Cycle. "Possibly as long as seven Cycles, it is hard to say with that particular drug." Further, it seemed fairly clear that in defining the drugs used and Borros's reaction to Stahlig's voice, Security had been interrogating him.

"'Interviewing' they call it," he said. "One of the effects of this drug is to submerge the will. In other words—"

"They were picking his brain."

"Attempting to, yes."

"What do you mean?"

"Well, these things are very tricky and they are certainly not foolproof."

"But why not just confiscate his notes? Surely that would have been easier."

The Medicine Man shrugged. "Perhaps they could not decipher them, who knows? In any event, most of what Freidal told us and allowed us to hear was false."

"But why go to all that trouble? And if what you say is true, that means Security has deliberately interfered in the work of a Magic Man."

"Quite so." Stahlig nodded. "And then there is the matter of the Dehn spots—" He stopped abruptly. They both heard soft footfalls in the darkness outside. He said in a louder voice: "Time is passing. It is near to Sehna." In an undertone, he added: "You must be at board. You understand?"

Ronin nodded.

"And tomorrow and tomorrow." Then louder: "Good, I shall see you later. I will need to take another look at that bruise." He flicked his eyes and, with the briefest movement of his head, Ronin again nodded. He rose and left. In the surgery he passed two daggam groping through the dark on their way to see Stahlig.

HE passed up the only working Lift in this Sector because the queue was far too long and he lacked the patience to wait. He was hailed several times and he smiled distractedly and raised a hand perfunctorily but he did not stop to greet anyone formally or to talk.

His body went on automatic, as it often did, so that he was only just aware of his surroundings. He was deep in thought but his body knew where to walk to get to the proper Stairwell leading Upshaft to his own Level.

Consequently, he went right by Nirren without seeing him. He was a tall, dark-complexioned man with an aquiline nose and deep-set eyes. He turned, not in the least surprised and, grabbing an arm impulsively, spun Ronin around. Ronin felt the shadow of the approach before the Chondrin had touched him, and there was no resistance in him. He spun with the momentum, and as he did so, he drew his sword with such lightning swiftness that his arm was no more than a blur. The blade was up and ready, light spilling along

27

its width, before he had even seen who had grasped him. Nirren's blade was barely out of its scabbard.

Nirren laughed, showing white, even teeth. "One day I swear I shall best you."

Ronin smiled bleakly and sheathed his sword. "Not a day for one of your tricks." The smile faded and died.

But the Chondrin was in good humor. His eyes widened and he said in a parody of a whisper: "Ah, secrets to share with your wise and witty friend." He put his arm around Ronin. "Tell all and unending happiness shall be yours."

Ronin thought fleetingly of Stahlig's admonition and was instantly annoyed with himself. There were questions that puzzled him and Nirren might have the answers to some of them. In any case, he was a friend. My only friend, he thought with a start.

He smiled. "All right. My quarters?"

They entered the Stairwell and Nirren lit a torch. "Double practice again today, eh?" He shook his head as they made their way Upshaft. "When are you going to be sensible and turn your mind to useful activity?"

Ronin grunted. "Such as?"

The Chondrin grinned. "Well, it just so happens there is a fine position under Jargiss—"

"I knew it—"

"Now wait, he is really all right, for a Saardin— quick, and a brilliant strategist. I know you would get along. And he knows the meaning of defense, too." This was a favorite topic of his. He never tired of sketching hypothetical battle plans, outlining tactics for attacker and defender. Given the choice of ground, he would say, the defender will triumph nine out of ten times, even with less men.

"I have never met a Saardin I liked," Ronin said.

"Tell me, have you ever met Jargiss?"

Ronin shook his head. "This is like a game with you. No, not to talk to. How many times do you have to hear it?"

Nirren shrugged and grinned. "I keep believing that one of these times you will ask to meet him."

Ronin reached out and touched the orange and brown chest bands strapped over the Chondrin's brown shirt. "I think not," he said very softly.

"Listen, if it's about the Salamander, you have to expect—"

"That is not it at all."

"If you do not mind my saying so, I believe it is."

They were both very still then, regarding each other unwaveringly in the uncertain, sparkling light. The reeds of the torch crackled softly and the minute clash of tiny paws on concrete sounded intermittently. The noises were remote, from another world. Somewhere, very far off, boots sounded and then faded. Darkness lapped at their feet.

At last Ronin heard himself say: "Perhaps you are right." And the surprise stayed with him long after they emerged onto his Level.

His quarters were actually two cubicles, considerably more space than that of any other Bladesman. Chondrin were allotted this much room; Saardin had of course quite a bit more.

K'reen was there when they arrived. Her thick, dark hair was up and coiffed for Sehna but she still wore her work clothes: close-fitting leggings, and shirt loose through the torso to deemphasize the body underneath, with light sleeves. She was tall, fully Ronin's height, with a long, graceful neck, generous mouth, and wide-set dark eyes. When they came in, she smiled and touched Ronin's hand.

He was momentarily surprised because she should have been either finishing up her work on the Med Training Level or in her own quarters dressing for Sehna.

She breezed past them, on her way out. "I spent too much time searching for these in my quarters"—she waved silver bracelets at them—"until I realized I had left them here." She stuck her tongue out at Nirren and he grinned. "Unless I run I will never make Sehna on time." She closed the door behind her.

Ronin crossed to a cabinet, reached out a flagon of wine and goblets, poured them both a drink. Already K'reen was gone from his mind.

They sat facing each other on low stools covered with fur. The harsh, white light of the Overheads washed over them, draining the color from their faces. Nirren sipped at his wine. Ronin's lay untouched at his feet. He told the Chondrin about his meeting with Freidal. The other's eyes flashed briefly.

"What do you think?"

Nirren stood and paced the small room. "I think I must find out why Freidal is so interested in that Magic Man."

"They claim he is mad."

"If that is so, perhaps they made him mad."

"But the spots."

Nirren turned. "What?"

"The marks on Borros's head."

"Ah, yes. The Dehn spots. That could have been it, you see. And all the more reason for me to find out what Freidal is planning as quickly as possible. Few people know of the Dehn. It is a machine of the Ancients. Like so many of the mysterious artifacts that keep us alive here—provide us with air and heat and light, more than three kilometers below the surface of the planet—we know only what it does; the *how* is beyond us." His voice took on a bitter edge. "Yet we have knowledge enough to use it. Wires are attached to the head—at the places where you saw the spots— and shocks are delivered to the brain by the same method by which our Overheads function. Do you remember the Neer who opened one up some time ago and touched the wrong wire? He was black when they found him, and he stank. They had a lot of trouble identifying him because his plate had melted." He sipped his wine and sat down again.

"In any event, the Dehn is very painful, so I am told. Consequently it can be quite reliable in obtaining information from recalcitrants. But there is trouble in controlling it; what can you expect when you are in the dark." He paused for a moment, lost in thought. "What *is* Freidal up to?"

Ronin felt something stir within him. He rose. "Let me understand this. Are you saying that the Saardin of Security has interfered in the work of a Magic Man, has—what, tortured him, to gain information that he will use for himself?"

Nirren stabbed a finger in the air and his eyes sparkled. "Precisely, my friend. I see there is hope for you yet. The time of battle draws nigh, and when it comes Freidal and Jargiss shall be on opposing sides. We are enemies, he and I." He grasped Ronin by the shoulders. "Listen, my friend, the time for neutrality has passed. All shall be affected by the struggle. You must help us. Ask Stahlig to talk to Borros while there is still time. It is the only way, I cannot get at Freidal quickly. And if we gain knowledge of his secret, it will give us much strength."

"Perhaps Freidal has learned nothing."

"I cannot afford to think that way."

Ronin looked at him. "You do not care what they have done to him. I do not even know whether he will be able to talk coherently after what they have subjected him to."

There was a warmth in Nirren's eyes. "Be realistic, my friend. I am talking about something that is larger than any one individual. We are all merely pieces. The Freehold is disintegrating before our eyes because of dissension among the Saardin. You are unaffiliated, so perhaps you are not so aware of it, but believe me when I tell you that much work must be done if we are to survive. But right now, no decisions are being made on behalf of the Freehold. You see? They are all too busy scheming to consolidate their power. This will cause our destruction."

"Perhaps it will be your battle which causes our destruction," said Ronin.

Nirren dropped his arms and made a face. "I will not argue with you. I debate with our people at every Spell, I do not come to you for this."

He grinned suddenly and gulped down the remainder of his wine. "Think on what I have said. I will say nothing further on the subject. I have sufficient trust in you. Agreed?"

Ronin smiled and shook his head. He thought: When he grins, his enthusiasm is hard to ignore. He made a mock bow. "As you wish."

Nirren laughed and rose. "Good. Then I will be off. I barely have enough time to change. Until Sehna, then."

Alone in his quarters, Ronin picked up his untouched wine and sipped it. It was cool and deliciously tart. It could have been brackish water for all he tasted it.

SEHNA. The evening meal. A sacred time. So many traditions, Ronin thought as he entered the Great Hall. And how many generations preceded us, lying now in dust, remembered by the traditions they handed down and nothing else.

The heat and noise hit him simultaneously, a vast kinetic wave, startling and bright. Continuous random motion. The Great Hall stretched away, its farthest reaches obscured by a haze of fragrant steam and smoke and heat. Long tables with low-backed benches filled with men and women proliferated in precise rows into the distance. Momentarily his hand strayed to his hip. It felt light and strange without the weight of his sword, but weapons of any kind were forbidden at board.

He moved to the right, then turned and strode down one of the narrow aisles. He wore soft cream-colored leggings and shirt; no Saardin used that color. Servers made room for him to pass, lifting huge trays laden with steaming food or tankards of thick ale, flagons of sweet, amber wine. He smelled the mingled aromas of foodstuffs, light perfumes, and thick sweat.

He came at length to his table and took his accustomed place between Nirren and K'reen. She was deep in conversation with a Bladesman next to her, so that he saw only the dark and shining helmet of her hair. He smelled her perfume. Across the table, Telmiss lifted a goblet in silent greeting, and next to him G'fand, a very young, blond man, was busy directing a Server.

"Well, how is our Scholar this Spell?" Ronin asked him.

G'fand turned and his blue eyes dropped under Ronin's gaze. "The same, I expect," he said softly.

Nirren laughed. "Now what could be the trouble this Cycle—lost one of your ancient manuscripts?" He laughed again and color rushed into G'fand's face. By this time K'reen had turned toward them, and, seeing the young man's discomfort, she reached out and covered his hand with hers. "Pay them no heed, they enjoy teasing you. They think swordsmanship is the most important skill in the Freehold."

"You have evidence to the contrary, my lady?" Nirren said formally, and grinned. "If so I should like to hear it."

"Quiet, you," she admonished.

G'fand said rather stiffly, as if no one would hear him: "It is all right. I expect it from him."

"And not from me?" Ronin leaned back as a Server filled his plate. He indicated that he wanted wine, not ale.

G'fand said nothing, his eyes still averted.

Ronin began to eat, his mind far away. "I shall endeavor, in the future, not to tease you."

At that moment Tomand and Bessat arrived. They were seated amid a great uproar from the table, partly because it amused them to make a fuss over Tomand's corpulence, partly because they felt they must ease the tension. Sehna was a time for relaxation, no matter what else was happening throughout the Freehold.

Slowly the table settled down and the food was served. Noise increased and the heat became oppressive. "Chill take me," Nirren said, "why is it so hot in here?"

Tomand stopped eating momentarily and, wiping his heavy, sweating jowls, gestured for him to lean forward. "Just between us," he glanced from Nirren to Ronin, "we are having problems with the ventilation system." He took another forkful of food. "In fact, that is why we were late to Sehna. We were working until the last moment, trying to figure out the cursed thing."

"With very little success, I notice," said Nirren.

Tomand grimaced. "It is simply impossible. We have lost too much knowledge." He chewed, then continued. "The most we can do is to try to clean up the mess. I mean how are we supposed to fix something if we don't know how it works? So little of what the Ancients wrote has survived. Only their Machines—"

"No," interrupted G'fand, "we could not destroy their Machines without destroying ourselves."

Tomand paused with a forkful of food halfway to his greasy lips. "What are you saying?"

"That the writings of the Ancients were deliberately destroyed in the early days of the Freehold."

Tomand shoved the fork into his mouth, and said around the food: "What nonsense. Who would willfully destroy knowledge? Certainly not civilized folk."

G'fand said carefully: "The Ancients invented many things. A number of them were quite lethal. And they were inveterate graphologers. It appears that our forefathers had little faith in those who would come after them. In any event, they took no chances. They destroyed the written wisdom of the Ancients. Destroyed it indiscriminately, so that I, a Scholar, cannot learn their history, and you, a Neer, cannot understand the workings of the Air Machines, and the Saardin cannot learn how to destroy each other and the Freehold."

Tomand wiped his mouth.

Nirren said: "How came you by this?"

"A fanciful story, that is all it is," sniffed Tomand. "A speech to impress us. Everyone knows—"

"What the Frost do you know anyway?" G'fand flared. "You cannot even perform your job!"

Tomand choked and began to cough. Bessat looked over in alarm as Telmiss thumped him on the back until the coughing subsided somewhat. His face was red and his eyes were tearing. "How—dare you!" was all he could manage to get out.

G'fand was rigid. "You fat slug! All you do is eat. You serve no useful function. All you Neers are alike, ineffectual and—"

"Enough!" Ronin said sharply. "I think you owe Tomand an apology." He knew it was the wrong approach as soon as he said it.

G'fand turned on him, eyes blazing. "Who are you to tell me anything!" His voice had risen, overtones of rage and hysteria combining. Cords stood out along his neck. He rose, his arms tense columns, fists tight clumps pressed whitely against the tabletop. "It is you who owe us an apology. You don't care a bit about us"—his arm swung in a tight arc—"*any* of us. Your training keeps you above all that." He was spitting the words out, and Ronin could tell without looking that heads at adjoining tables were beginning to turn in their direction. But the myriad minute motions of the Great Hall had faded like a painting exposed to the rays of the sun. The hundreds of conversations and separate lives had ceased to exist.

"G'fand—" K'reen began, but he swept on without even noticing.

"You're special because the Salamander took you and trained you. For what? To sit here with the likes of us, without the affiliation of a Saardin? He must be sorely disappointed in you!"

Ronin sat impassively, and allowed it to flow past him. Even so, he was abruptly thinking of K'reen, her white skin. And then he saw quite clearly the face of a man strapped to a bed, two smudgy triangles high on his temples. He could hear screaming, a terrible pain-filled noise.

Consequently he did not move fast enough to completely avoid G'fand's mad lunge across the table. Plates and goblets burst apart, sending their contents showering in all directions as they tumbled over backward into the narrow aisle. Servers scattered and people along the adjacent row were sent reeling into their own tables.

G'fand tried to yell but all that came out were grunts as he pummeled the body beneath him. For his part, Ronin was of two minds, as he defended himself.

He did not want to hurt the Scholar but neither did he wish to prolong the scuffle and thus risk the intervention of Security daggam. Then, as G'fand shifted, a knee caught him in the side and he felt the lattice of pain lance up into his shoulder. The breath went out of him and he thought, Should have had Stahlig bandage the thing. And the instinct of his training took over. He lashed out with his free hand, slamming his fist into G'fand just below his ear. The Scholar's eyes bulged and his head danced like that of a puppet. Ronin took a breath and, in that instant, felt a searing pain. He twisted his head, saw the hilt of a small dagger protruding from his shoulder, tore it out, cursing, heard dimly the clatter as he dropped it, balled his hand, and swung into G'fand's midriff at the low point of the sternum. He had a momentary glimpse of the other's eyes, open wide, terror burning in them like an uncontrollable fire, before he doubled over. Ronin felt the spurt of adrenaline and he became aware that his fist was raised again. Then he was in control, panting, sweat stinging his eyes, hearing the strange sound of G'fand vomiting onto the floor. He touched him on his bowed back. With that came an understanding of what he had done, and what he had almost done. Then he swung about, searching for the dagger.

Nirren was beside him. "I had better see about poor G'fand," he said softly. Ronin nodded. He put his palm up to his shoulder because it was still numb and he would not feel the pain for a while, but he wanted to stop the blood.

Then he felt K'reen behind him, and she knelt and he saw her face. Wisps of hair had come undone so that she looked as if she had been standing in a high wind. Her cheeks were slightly flushed, her lips parted. Down deep in the awful stillness at the core of his being, he felt an inexplicable movement, as if he were a stringed instrument and something he could not see had plucked a thawed chord. He shivered involuntarily and K'reen, misunderstanding, put an arm across his shoulders. He shrugged it off, and she crouched like that, very quickly, so that only he could see, bent her head, flash of pink tongue, and licked at the crack between two of his fingers at the oozing strip of blood. He stood up then, but not before he had seen her eyes shining.

"Clear away! Clear away!" called a commanding voice. The gaping crowd parted reluctantly and Ronin saw two daggam push their way toward him. Someone at the fringe of the crowd must have summoned them. He cursed silently and wished he knew where G'fand's dagger was. They came up to him. If they found it—

"What caused the disruption?" The one who was not talking stood with his hands free. There was some space around him. Neither of them bothered to look at G'fand as Nirren helped him to his feet.

Ronin took a deep breath, let it go slowly. "Nothing at all," he said calmly. "Just a slight misunderstanding."

The daggam grunted. "Huh! Awful lotta people staring at a 'slight misunderstanding.' "

"You know how people are."

"Yeh, sure. Listen, you Bladesmen know better than to disrupt the Sehna. You got a problem, go work it out at the Hall of Combat, not here. Get me?"

Ronin nodded. "Sure."

The other one had not moved at all. He stood

watching Ronin. His eyes looked opaque, as if they had been painted on. "Names," said the one who talked, and Ronin gave them while he wrote. Then he took down Ronin's account of the argument.

"What happened to your shoulder?" asked the other one, and the first one looked up.

"I was getting to that," he said, with some annoyance.

"Wanted to make sure, is all," said the other.

"Well?" The stylus was poised.

"I must have cut it on the edge of a plate when I fell. Quite a lot of them broke."

"Yeh, so I see." He turned. "All right, nothing going on here," he called to the crowd, and they began to disperse. "Go on," he told the other one, and as he turned to leave, he said to Ronin: "Clean up this mess."

K'reen stood silently beside Ronin, her hand on his back. He looked at Nirren, who shook his head. "I can manage." He still had to support G'fand almost totally. "Look after yourself."

Ronin nodded. He turned and saw Tomand, face white and sweaty. Bessat was comforting him as if he were a small child. They came up to him and Tomand said, "I do not know what to—" He eyed the blood. "But he had it coming to him."

"It was about time someone stopped that kind of talk," said Bessat. "We are grateful."

Ronin felt annoyed. "That is simply what it was. Talk. He meant none of it."

"He insulted me all right," whined Tomand. "But he feels differently about it now, I'll warrant."

Very softly K'reen said: "I had better clean you up. Now."

Ronin looked at her. She had recognized the drift of the conversation.

"Yes." He sighed. "I suppose you had better."

"AND no one saw you pick it up?"

"I rather think not. They were all too busy."

"Yes. I can see that."

"How far did it go in?"

"To the hilt."

He sat on the bed, with his shirt off, turning G'fand's dagger over and over in his open palm, staring at the blade with its dark smear. K'reen bent over him, working on the wound. Occasionally she rummaged in an open bag beside her.

They had gone at first to Stahlig's, even though he knew it could have been awkward. But the surgery was dark and the cubicle behind it, and there was no telling where the Medicine Man had gone or when he would return. So they had come to K'reen's quarters because of her bag.

She began to stitch the wound closed, having already cleaned it thoroughly. "What is wrong with that boy? A weapon at Sehna! What was he thinking of?"

He kept his body very still. "He is not a boy, firstly,"

he said. "And he takes his work seriously—perhaps too seriously. They do not exactly make it easy for the Scholars, and it affects him. Perhaps." He forgot and shrugged.

"Keep still." Her hands were suddenly motionless, then began again.

"I do know that what I said to Tomand is true: he meant none of it." She finished the stitching and laid a dressing over it.

"But he attacked you."

"Yes," said Ronin, "and that is what bothers me."

She took cream from the bag and began to massage it onto the bruise over his ribs, which was slightly swollen, with the skin turned dark colors.

"Why?"

He shrugged.

"Do you really care?"

He said nothing. Her fingers felt good against his skin. Along the ridge of swollen flesh she tenderly stroked the inflamed muscles. She wondered what he was thinking about, fancied it was her. She wiped her hands, and unbound her hair so that it fell thick as a forest, long, swirling about her pale face. Traces of the cream glistened in her hair, iridescent and unreal. Her fingers scooped into the bag, came out, set to work again.

"I had never seen you fight before," she said softly. And something in her voice recalled the image: swift pink tongue on bright scarlet. He flung the dagger from him so that it cartwheeled in a bright arc and stuck in the floor, quivering. He turned his hands over, staring at the backs, fingers clenched, knuckles white. He slammed them together.

"It's all right," she whispered.

The adrenaline was not quite gone. "I am trained," he said slowly and softly, "to kill and to stay alive. All Bladesmen learn this, some better than others. But those years with the Salamander were different, and now there are times when instinct takes over—very pure and very lethal—because there is no time to think: *Hesitate and you are dead.*" He paused and spread his hands, and, perhaps, at that moment he was not aware of her at all. "I almost killed him—it was so close. He was defenseless and terrified at what he had done."

"I know," she said.

His back arched slightly as he felt her breasts press into him as she leaned over. Her fingers worked. "To see you in Combat," she whispered at his ear. "I want that." She moved her hands up to the nape of his neck and began a circular motion that drew the tension from his tired muscles. "I think about that."

"Somehow I cannot imagine you spending your free time that way." His body relaxed.

She moved her breasts from side to side against his back. "I am full of surprises," she said with a light laugh. Then her fingers moved down along his spine, slowly circling. The stroking became rhythmic. "Do you win?"

"Yes. All the time." He was aware that she very much wanted to hear him say it. It was something she already knew.

Her fingers moved lower and again he felt her presence more closely. He breathed her perfume. Strands of her unbound hair brushed lightly against him in concert with her hands. He heard breathing in the silence of their attenuated conversation; became aware that it was his own as well as hers.

Her fingers were at the base of his spine; she touched the tops of his buttocks. Her lips were so near his ear that he could feel her warm breath. "You fought magnificently. You fought and you bled and through it all I was thinking of only one thing." Her fingers made wider circles on his body; the pressure more insistent.

He felt his blood pounding. He said nothing.

Her lips touched his ear. They were moist, and she made a sound.

He twisted then, oblivious to his pains, and pulled her into his lap. His hands were lost in the night forest of her hair, clung there. He pressed his lips savagely against hers. Her mouth opened. His hands moved slowly, sinuously down her body, and she moaned into his mouth. And he reached for the fastening of her robe.

THEY were thin and tall and quite young. The hilts of the triple daggers across their gray shirts shone dully in the cold lights of the Overheads, still in reasonably good condition this far Upshaft. One said: "Freidal wishes to see you." He seemed very sure of the identification, although Ronin had seen neither of them before.

He felt a brief worry as he thought of Borros. It was very early, first Spell had not half gone, and he was back on his own Level. They had gotten him as he had walked to his quarters, appearing abruptly from around the far turning, stepping in front of him before he reached his door. Important to remember, he thought, in this Stahlig was right: Freidal is very dangerous.

"At once," the daggam said.

Security had an entire Sector Upshaft. He had never been there, but for as long as he could remember there had been stories told and retold along

47

the Corridors Up- and Downshaft of the strange and secretive doings there. He had automatically discounted most of that talk; now he was not so sure.

He was surprised, however, to find that the forbidding dull gray exterior, with its massive doors and gates manned by faultlessly garbed daggam, gave way to quarters remarkably bland in appearance. Cubicles that were lit contained daggam pursuing innocuous functions: stacking tablets, desk work, and such. They passed many rooms dark and empty. Some were clearly storage areas, others obviously not, and this was puzzling. A door opened on his right and a daggam emerged. Behind him a glimpse in pale, flickering light of a central table with something pinned on top: scored lines. The door closed swiftly and they moved on. Image remaining: heavy shadows, many daggam. And what was on the table?

"In here." They went through a doorway into a small cubicle lit by Overheads. "Wait here." The daggam left him through a large door. Blank gray walls stared back at him dispassionately. Two chairs, bare floor. Dark shapes moving over the table, pointing. He waited, conscious of fatigue and the dull throbbing in his shoulder. He badly wanted to wash, and he was hungry.

The door opened and a daggam emerged. Eyes the color of mud regarded him with dull antipathy: Marcsh. Deliberate, Ronin wondered, or is he part of the Saardin's personal staff? Marcsh cocked his thumb at the door. "In," he said laconically.

Ronin said, "What else do you do besides stand at doors?" because he was tired and annoyed.

Marcsh's animal eyes squinted as he made a face. "Least I got a Saardin."

Ronin advanced. "To give you orders."

"'Course. What else?" His jaw clenched. "Orders is what counts, good orders. An' we got 'em." Ronin was very close now. "That's why we—" Marcsh's eyes got cunning.

"You what?"

"Nuthin'." He went sullen. "Just got my orders. Make sure you behave."

Is that so. Ronin stepped around him and into the room. The door closed behind him, as Marcsh pulled it shut. It was deep gray with very murky Overheads. No carpet, but two unusual wall hangings in dark, muted colors. An ornate desk cut the cubicle off obliquely. Behind it, in a high-backed chair, sat Freidal. He was dressed as before, in dark gray. Silver chest bands glittered. A large lighted lamp squatted on a low cabinet behind him, so it was difficult to see the features of his face. The Overheads illuminated only the top of his head. He did not look up. Across from him sat the scribe, tablet crooked on arm, quill poised. He seemed oblivious to anything except the spoken word. There was one chair before the desk. Ronin ignored it.

After a time, Freidal shuffled some sheets, put aside a scroll, and raised his head.

"Sir?"

The scribe's left hand moved, a tiny scratching.

"You sent for me," Ronin said in an even tone.

"Ah yes, so I did." He did not ask Ronin to sit down. The false eye was white and terrible in the reflected bright light. "You had better tell me all about it."

"I do not—"

"You most certainly do," snapped the Saardin, "know very well." The scribe's hands made patterns on the tablet. "Begin, sir." Freidal's hands were perfectly still, clasped together on the desktop, white blobs of color. Except for the unblinking eye, his face was a shadow, unreadable. Ronin thought furiously.

"An argument—"

"I do not believe you, sir."

But at least he had gotten it right. "All right," he said resignedly. "I had hoped this would be passed over, but—well, remarks were made about the Salamander, about—"

"One finds it difficult to believe you are so thin-skinned." A white hand flicked and light caught the polished nails.

What does he want to hear? A bit of the truth, perhaps. "We—did not part on the best of terms, as you no doubt know." Sweat had begun to break out on his forehead, and that was good. "Many think, therefore, that they may insult him, believing that it will please me. But he was my Sensii and I owe him a great deal."

There was a pause and Ronin knew that the Saardin was referring to the report. "He made numerous—unhealthy remarks," Freidal said.

"Who did?"

"The Scholar."

"I do not—"

"Other people have given witness."

This is such a minor matter. What is he interested in? "Under the circumstances, I should think the Saardin would understand."

"You are defending him?"

Careful. "He is quite harmless, Saardin. He is, after all, a Scholar."

The papers rustled. "One cannot be too careful," the Saardin said pedantically, "when it comes to Tradition. Such a disturbance at Sehna is cause for an investigation, I am sure you understand that. Order must be maintained at all costs—at any cost. Sehna is the time of obeisance to the Saardin and thus to the Freehold itself. Without the Freehold's structure, we are nothing. Without Tradition, discipline, order, we become barbarians. You understand this clearly, sir?" The hands separated, spread themselves upon the desktop, an implicit threat. "I am aware that you are without affiliation. Is that one of the principles you were taught Upshaft?" The eye winked out for a moment, shone again. "One wonders, sir, what the Salamander would think of one of his pupils—pardon me—ex-pupils who was involved in a disturbance at Sehna." His tongue clicked against the roof of his mouth.

His head turned then, just enough so that Ronin could see that he was smiling. "I am most apologetic at having to disturb you so early, but"—he shrugged— "the routines of Security must be maintained." The white eye winked out as he looked down again. He moved papers off to the side, seemed to be studying something.

"You forgot your sword," he said.

Ronin almost said something then, but understanding came just in time. He stood very still and stared at the shiny cap of the Saardin's hair. Far off a door slammed, and nearer, booted feet tramped down a hallway, setting a cadence.

"There's a good boy," said the Saardin. And Ronin

knew he was angry, felt some small satisfaction. The sounds of the boots faded, and the silence came again. His shoulder ached.

"That is your own business." The Saardin's head came up, flash of white light. "Other things are *my* business." His voice took on a pedantic tone again. "Do you know why Security was created, sir? For two reasons. One: to protect the Freehold from invasion from the Outside. Two: to protect the Freehold from those within who would seek to destroy it." His hands steepled before him, fingers interlaced like white blades. "Now we are the last. The earth above us is frozen solid and no one can survive there. All other Freeholds perished long ago. Perished because they forsook the Traditions. Perished because they lacked our discipline, sir.

"And so we are the last. And by the Chill, I shall ensure that we remain and flourish." The hands came apart. "While there is no one from Above who can harm us, there are still members of the Freehold, hiding among us, who wish us ill." The hands came down hard on the desktop. "That I will not tolerate! Do you understand me, sir?" Ronin· nodded. "Good. Very good."

He turned suddenly in his chair and pointed behind him at a wall hanging. "You see this? A fine piece of work. Excellent. Better than anything we can do. How old do you estimate it is? Hmm? Two hundred years, three? A millennium. At least. What do you think of that? And we do not have the faintest idea who made it. What kind of people, even. Could have been our forefathers. Perhaps not. No records. Very mysterious, yes?" He turned back. "There are many mysteries within the Freehold. Most people do not know about them. No time. Would not care about them, if they did. Then there are those few people who cannot resist poking around things they have no business being near. They get hurt that way."

A small silence built itself in the room and the air seemed to get thick and difficult to breathe. "I trust you have good sense."

The white eye went out once more as Freidal returned to his papers. The scratching of the quill had ceased. After a time, the Saardin said, without looking up, "Sir, I believe you are late for Combat practice."

E̷XTEND the leg twist block thrust forward and down. All in one motion. Return to position. This one will never make it, he thought, as his opponent bent to retrieve the sword he had just flicked out of his hand. No more than a blur.

Not far away Nirren *posted*, a deceptively slow movement, which his opponent reacted to, making him vulnerable to the difficult *solenge*, which Nirren executed with terrifying speed. The point of his blade hooked, bit and thrust, and it was over. Ronin wiped his forehead with the side of his wrist as he watched Nirren step back and bow to his opponent.

Black shadows moving slowly around a table, orange flame flickering, sending shards of light glinting from deadly dagger hilts.

The din of two hundred men boomed off the walls of the Hall of Combat. The place reeked of sweat, hanging heavily on the hazy air. Ronin could not allow himself to miss practice, although he wanted to see Stahlig. He felt instinctively that he must maintain his routine as much as possible. He did not take Freidal's warning lightly.

All eyes on the table in the center of the room: lines drawn in a familiar pattern. But there had been no time. He had just a split second and he had not been looking directly at the tabletop. The pattern had registered on the periphery of his vision, so that now he could not force it, it would have to surface on its own.

Nirren walking over, very little sweat on him. He grinned. "How about a real workout?" Ronin smiled, bowed to his opponent, turned to face Nirren. They took up position, searching for an opening.

On the other hand, he had no more doubts as to his course of action. In fact it was the Saardin's warning that had decided him. Not that he had ignored his friend's plea. But in the end it was because this very powerful and dangerous man with the false eye and the smile of a cold animal had warned him away, that he was going to find out all he could about Borros, the mad Magic Man. The authority principle: it rankled.

Nirren found it first, and Ronin, his reaction time down because his mind had been elsewhere, was hard pressed to turn the attack aside: the *faeas*, low thrust, blade extended far forward, flicking up at the last instant, ready to disembowel, and if it was successful, that was the end. Ronin did the only thing he could, turning sideways and plunging his blade straight down just in front of his forward thigh. It was instinct and speed. The inexperienced Bladesman would retreat and that would be it. Attack the *faeas*. Their blades clanged sharply and Ronin swung immediately out and up, attempting to take advantage of Nirren's extension

—the drawback of the *faeas* if it does not work—but the Chondrin countered.

By the end of practice, Ronin had disadvantaged Nirren twice, but, as usual, neither had gained a decisive victory. But then neither was looking for victory. They had been trained differently and thus had vastly individual styles. In practice they learned from each other, keeping their reflexes sharp and their minds ready for the unexpected. Ronin knew many tricks that he simply would not use during a practice; he supposed Nirren had some too.

Into the Corridor and on the way Upshaft, the tarred reeds fitfully illuminating the scarred and cracked concrete walls of the Stairwell. Patterns of lines rippling past him, and he had it, the latent image impressed through the retina onto the brain suddenly given meaning.

When Nirren had asked him to have a drink after practice he had declined, thinking of Stahlig and Borros. Now he wanted a talk with the Chondrin.

His quarters were much like Ronin's several Levels Upshaft: two sparsely furnished cubicles. "Sirreg's not in, so we need not worry about what we say," Nirren told him, reaching out a flagon and goblets from a cabinet. They drank the deep red wine, their sweat drying, muscles relaxing. Ronin sat back in the cushions of the divan, feeling the spreading warmth within him. "I have never asked you this, but how did you become affiliated?"

Nirren looked at him reflectively and sipped his wine. "You mean the belief?" He cocked his head.

"Um, so it is not true what they say about you?" He said it with a smile.

"You know perfectly well what is true and what is not."

"What ever gave you that idea?" He shook his head. "My friend, there are many stories—perhaps because you have so few friends, perhaps because you are unaffiliated—they cannot understand that—"

"Neither can you," said Ronin not unkindly.

"Ah, not true, my friend. Your choice. I respect that, but—well, one must try—"

"If one has the belief."

Nirren shrugged. "Or not. Many do not have it, deep down. But the world of the Saardin is all they know. In any event, they fear you—yes, fear is the correct term—because you are a mystery. That and the Salamander, of course. They believe you shun them because of some terrible deed you once committed. Very interesting. But I digress. You asked how I became affiliated." He refilled the goblets. "Very well then.

"When I was a Student I had a friend, never mind his name, and he was very ambitious. He dreamed of becoming a Chondrin and thence a Saardin. Now the world is a complete place—you and I understand that now—my friend did not. He craved power but refused to acknowledge the Traditional paths to that end. I saw what was happening, and although I had no clear idea of the world at that time, still I knew down here"—he pointed to his stomach—"that he was wrong in his approach. I spoke to him but he would not listen. He nodded his head, said 'Yes, that is good advice,' and then went out and did the opposite."

His voice had taken on overtones, the words hanging vividly in the air. He sipped his wine and regarded Ronin. "And then one Spell we filed into the Hall for practice. We found him spread out on the floor in the shape of a star. Five points in a dark and evil-smelling pool: head, arms, and legs. And none of them connected."

He finished off his wine, poured them both more. It was very quiet in the cubicle; outside, the Corridor was still.

Ronin cleared his throat. "And then?"

"And then I knew I must affiliate myself as quickly as possible."

"After what you saw?"

"Precisely that, yes. One moment he was there, full of life and bluff disregard for the Traditions of the world, the next—nothing. A mote of matter. They had gone through him, discarded him as if he were a pile of rubble they had hauled from here to there. The results were public so that we should not mistake his death. They wanted us to know.

"I saw very clearly what I must do. I am a realist, my friend. I understood what he wanted. He was not an evil man. And he was right to want power. Without it we are nothing; worse, we achieve nothing. Power is the link between dream and reality. He understood its nature as do I. But he lacked foresight and patience, and he paid for those deficiencies. I do not mourn for him.

"The world is reality, any fool can see that. One does not have to agree with it, but one must allow oneself to work *within* its structure, do you see. To obtain the power. From there, anything is possible, my friend. Anything." He was finished and Ronin knew he was waiting for a response.

Nirren rose and went to the cabinet for another flagon. As if divining Ronin's thoughts he said: "I do not expect anything from you. I want that quite clear."

"Why say it?"

Nirren smiled then. "Are you surprised that I should tell you all this?"

Ronin shook his head. "You know the answer to that."

The Chondrin laughed. "My friend, I know you not at all."

"Because you know nothing of my background. Is that so important?"

"A man is forged by his background, Ronin," Nirren said with some force. "And you are only fooling yourself if you believe otherwise."

"All of us are different."

"Aye, up to a point."

"At the center, I mean. At the core of the being."

"At the center all men are linked by their spirit."

Ronin looked at him with dark eyes. "Do you really believe that?"

"Yes."

He said very softly, "I am not," and it rushed at him on a chill wind down deep where he feared to go, and knew not why he felt a rushing in his ears and a wetness on his face and body, pinpoints of pressure, and very far off a gasping sound distorted and inexplicably terrifying, and he tried to see but something was in his eyes like mist, so that nothing was clear, and . . .

"—do you know?" Nirren was asking. He leaned over to pour more wine. Ronin cleared his throat again, put his hand over the top of his goblet. "Enough," he said thickly.

Nirren laughed. "Aha, yes. I believe you are right. Too early for more." He stopped the flagon, put it away, turned. "You did not answer."

"What?"

"Did you know that Jargiss is my second affiliation?"

"No, I—"

"It does not often happen. That is, not many are able to break affiliation and live."

Wisp of mist, still. "But you did."

"Yes, but I was lucky. Jargiss knew of me, my situation, and he approached me."

"Who was the first?"

"Ah. Dharsit."

The Chondrin's skin like wax, white scar pulling at one eye, colors of black and gold. He told Nirren of the incident.

"Just like his Saardin. I am not surprised. They treat Combat without respect. They are Freidal's men."

"But he is such a Traditionalist."

"Yes, but it does not matter. He uses them only. After he is finished with them—he will use Dharsit's men first in battle, they will make the first assault and they will die—both Saardin and Chondrin will cease to exist."

"I saw Freidal today," said Ronin. "He sent for me."

Nirren went very still. "Really." His tone was neutral but as Ronin related what had happened he could see that the Chondrin was excited.

Nirren frowned. "Either he is being overly cautious, or he has some interest in you. I do not like it."

"I saw something while I was at Security. A room filled with daggam studying a large tablet. I only got the briefest glance but I am sure now. They were looking at a map."

Nirren did not move and his face was lit by a tense concentration. He said: "You could not be mistaken?"

"No."

He nodded. "Very well. Anything else you can remember? Details of the map—"

Ronin shook his head.

The Chondrin sat back for a moment, then stood up. "Come," he said. "We shall go to Jargiss."

"There are other matters that require my attention."

They were at the door. Nirren knew better than to press it. "Later, then."

"Yes," said Ronin. "Later."

BECAUSE of his shoulder wound, he felt confident in approaching Stahlig, even if his visit was reported to Freidal. Sirreg was just coming out of the Medicine Man's quarters when he arrived. His brown and orange shirt was stained and one arm was bandaged near the wrist. "Ronin. Good to see you." He was blond with a fine, square face and direct, dark eyes with long lashes. His face darkened. "I heard what happened at Sehna." He shook his head. "What are we coming to. Brawls at Sehna, really!"

Ronin pointed. "What happened to you?" He had no wish to discuss the fight, especially in the Corridor.

Sirreg grimaced. "A souvenir from one of Dharsit's Bladesmen." He laughed shortly. "It is nothing, really. You should see what I left with *him*."

"This happened in Combat?"

"No, in the Corridor—Downshaft. One must get used to these inconveniences now." He shook his head again. "But at Sehna! Would that I had seen it. Nirren

62

has all the best of it, being able to sit at any board he chooses, while we Bladesmen are stuck—have you seen him this Spell by chance?"

"He was off to see Jargiss not a few moments ago."

"Ah. Well, then." He lifted his good arm and walked.

A Neer was waiting to see Stahlig when Ronin entered. She was neither attractive nor unattractive, with short brown hair and a lined face like a ripe fruit. She stared at him unashamedly. "I don't get to see many Bladesmen," she said in a thin dry voice. "That's because I'm Downshaft at the eighty-fifth Level." Ronin had never met anyone who had been that far Downshaft. "Huge Machines Down there—larger than you can imagine, I'll warrant." She began to stroke her leg and Ronin saw that the foot and ankle were bandaged. There seemed to be something wrong with the foot's angle to the leg.

She saw where he was looking. "In one of them," she said. "Frost, it hurt!" Her shoulders slumped. "We were working on one of the Air Machines—the primary ones, you know?—and they tell us first thing when we go Down there to mind the Machine fluids because they're slippery. I guess that's what happened. I stumbled and slid along the hot metal and"—her face screwed up—"oh, it was awful, the foot in the Machine! It took them almost an entire Spell to decide what to do and get me out." She stroked the shin above the mangled foot, not looking at it. "After a while I couldn't feel anything at all, so I didn't care when they talked about sending for a Medicine Man to cut off the foot. They were afraid of damaging the Machine in some way, because we still don't know how it works or even why, only that it does and keeps us alive." She smiled a beatific smile. "But in the end they managed to get it out by breaking the ankle and it was all right."

Stahlig came out to help her into the surgery and she looked back over her shoulder at him for as long as she could. He had never shared the Bladesman's contempt for Neers and Scholars and, of course, the Workers. Frost, it was not their fault, and someone had to—

Stahlig called him. There were several exits from the surgery and, for an obscure reason, Ronin was glad that the Neer had been sent another way. He went through the half-lit deserted surgery, the elliptical stone slab dominating the room. Its polished top and sloping pebbled sides caught the orange lamplight in such a way that for a startling moment it seemed to him to be covered with bright glistening blood, pooling thickly in the slight hollows of the top, running in complex networks down its sides. He blinked and looked again, saw light purple-gray stone marbleized with white striations. He moved slowly past high cases, into the inner cubicle.

If anything the clutter had increased. Stahlig was on the couch, sorting tablets of all sizes. "Mind those," he said as Ronin removed a pile from a chair.

"How long have you been treating Neers?"

The Medicine Man waved a hand. "Ah, they are overworked Downshaft. We—" He fought to keep the tablets from sliding off his lap, finally gave it up and dropped them to the floor. "We are expected to handle everything Up here without a word of complaint, otherwise they think we are getting ideas." He used his hands to brush off his leggings. "I heard about the mess at Sehna. That is just the kind of notice you do not need now. What happened? Take off your shirt."

As Ronin told him, Stahlig took apart the bandage and inspected the wound. "That idiot Scholar!" he said with annoyance. "Of course he is frustrated. They burned all his books centuries ago." With great care he worked a cream onto the area. "Mine too, for that matter, only—Who worked on this for you?" He looked up quickly, then went back to the shoulder. "Not much for me to do here, just put on a new dressing and in several Cycles you will not even know it is there."

"K'reen did it." Why did he have to ask? "We came by after Sehna but you were not here."

"Uhm, no. As I have said, they are giving me the overflow, and—" He shrugged. "Were the daggam called? At Sehna, I mean."

"Yes, but it was nothing. They took down a statement."

He seemed relieved. "Good. At least Freidal did not summon you."

Ronin thought: He seems changed. "But he did summon me—very early, during first Spell."

Sweat had come out on the Medicine Man's broad forehead. "I told you! By the Frost you were warned!"

"Calm yourself." Stahlig was finished with the dressing and Ronin stood up. "He only wanted to corroborate the daggam's report. What is the matter with you?"

Stahlig turned and went behind his desk. There was no color in his face. "I want you to forget you ever went with me yesterday." He stared at Ronin, his rheumy eyes sunken and worn. A tablet slipped off the desk and fell to the floor with a muffled crash. He did not appear to notice. "It never happened."

There was silence in the room, but still he was pleading.

"I cannot."

"Oh, Frost!" Ronin might just as well have hit him. His face crumpled and he collapsed onto the couch. His lips trembled. Ronin went and got some wine, knelt in front of him, made him drink it.

After a while he whispered, "I know you. I can do no more." But it was as if he were talking to himself.

"Stahlig," Ronin said softly. "You must help me. I want to talk to Borros."

"How can you ask me to help you to die?" His voice was feeble and there was no resolve behind it.

"I will not die," Ronin said carefully, because he had to make Stahlig understand. "And this may be very important for the Freehold. Remember the talk we had?"

He sat up at last and looked into Ronin's eyes. "Why do you wish to do this?" But it worked and the answer did not matter now.

Ronin shrugged.

"But you must have a reason!"

"How can I tell you when I do not know what it is myself?"

The old man sighed and shook his head. "I knew," he said sadly. "I knew all along." He stood and turned away. "Come back after Sehna. I need to look at that shoulder again."

At that moment he experienced an acute and inexplicable sense of loss. "Stahlig. I—"

The Medicine Man raised his hand. "Mind the tablets on the way out."

"**E**NTER."

The door remained closed, and the soft knocking came again. He set down his wine, went across the room, and opened it. G'fand stood there, head down. Ronin could see the bandage across his chest under the shirt.

"I—" He cleared his throat. "I am not disturbing you?"

"Not at all, I was just thinking of—"

"Because if I am, I can—"

He touched the Scholar. "Come in." G'fand seemed rooted to the spot and Ronin had to draw him inside. "Sit. Please." He crossed the room and picked up something from the top of a low table. "I was about to return this to you." He held it out.

G'fand shrank from it as if it were alive. "I never want to see that thing again!" he cried.

Ronin set the dagger down next to him. "Ah, but someday it may save your life."

G'fand broke down then and sobbed into his hands.

Ronin poured him some wine and this too he set beside him. At length G'fand stopped and his hands came away. "I am so ashamed," he said.

Ronin sat across from him. "And I too," he said quietly.

G'fand's head came up. A light came back to his eyes. "You? What have you to be ashamed of?"

He held out his hands. "I am a Bladesman. But, as you pointed out at Sehna, I have studied with the Salamander." Spots of color stood out on G'fand's cheeks. "I learned many skills from him, many techniques few other Bladesmen know. You see, I almost killed you—with these."

G'fand stared at his hands. "But I thought Combat is with the sword and the dagger."

"Combat is very ancient and has many layers."

"Yes, I see." G'fand knelt. "Oh, Ronin, I am so sorry. Please forgive me."

"Pick up your dagger and put it away."

The Scholar wiped his face. "I want you to know what happened."

"G'fand, I know that you were not attacking me."

Surprise, relief, puzzlement, all flickered across his face. "But how? I was not sure myself what I was doing."

Ronin smiled. "Yet it was quite apparent to me that you were extremely upset, and not by any of the things you were saying."

Color crept into his face again. "I am in your debt." He was silent for a moment. staring into the depths of his wine. He had not touched it, and now he picked up the goblet and sipped at it. It meant more to him than taking a drink.

"I will tell you something," he said slowly, "although it is very difficult for me. I have envied you for a long time, wanting to be a Bladesman and not—not having the chance." He laughed nervously. "I suppose I am too small in any event." He brought the goblet to his lips again, a swift convulsive movement, as if activity were a necessity now. "I yearn to know how we came to be as a people—and what took place before us. They were a great people, centuries ago, and they built many Machines—huge and awesome." He put the wine down, gripped himself at the elbows as if he were cold. "That is all beyond us now. We have lost everything. But I have reached a—I have read all that remains, that meager pile of knowledge."

His voice lowered. "They do not know it, but I have partially deciphered the glyphs of the very ancient writing that comes from the time when all people were surface dwellers. But it is not nearly enough, just odd fragments—it is nothing, really. I have been able to read just enough to know what an unforgivable thing they did."

He broke off and wrung his hands. He had not yet said what he had come to say. "So I thought after all I have chosen to be something that is worthless. Oh, I have grown used to the taunts—I had work to keep me busy. But now I have read everything, so they tell me."

He took out the dagger, watched light play along its stubby blade. "So some time ago I went to Combat practice"—he lifted his head, half afraid that Ronin would laugh—"just like that. The Students joked about it at first and made fun of me, and finally, when I kept coming, wanted to throw me out. But in the end the Instructor came over and gave me this and a short sword and said that since I was trying so hard at least I should have some weapons. And now I work with the Novices, but"—his head sunk again—"I know I will never be a Bladesman."

"There are other things to be," said Ronin.

"Nirren says nothing is as important."

"Nirren enjoys teasing you, but you must not believe everything he says."

"He is a Chondrin and he does not see!" G'fand blurted suddenly.

"See what?"

"That we are dying. *You* cannot see it? You heard Tomand. He does not know the workings of the Machines, no Neer does. Yet the Great Machines are all that keep us alive. The Instructor talks to us of Traditions, the Code of Combat. But what good are Traditions if the air fails or the food goes or no more water comes to us?"

He stood abruptly. "I cannot stand it! I do not want to remain here. There is nothing for me, nothing for anyone. And soon—soon the banner of Tradition shall wave over our rotting bones!"

THEY went to Sehna together and that seemed to settle everything. There was an awkward moment until Tomand stood and said, "You are forgiven, this is Sehna after all." Nirren looked at them and smiled to himself, and K'reen squeezed G'fand's hand.

There was much laughter and spirited talk amongst the group, but a lot of it had a hard brittle edge; the topics of conversation were of little consequence. And as the courses came and went and the wine flagon was emptied and refilled, they were gripped by a kind of desperation that caused their laughter to ring louder, as if noise and tumult would keep them safe from their inner thoughts.

Ronin understood this early on, and, while he ate and drank and laughed with the rest because any other course would have been suspect, this knowledge only deepened the gloom that had settled upon him. The Neer's story had started it, he supposed, and he cursed her and then himself. What does it matter to me? he thought angrily. Not my concern.

A Bladesman wearing orange and brown wove his way toward them. He bowed to his Chondrin, whispered briefly in his ear. Nirren nodded and leaned over to Ronin. "Estrille," he mouthed silently, rose, and made his excuses to the table.

In some way, although it might have been coincidental, his departure was the signal for even greater revelry. Tomand called to the adjacent tables and soon they were exchanging wine flagons and goblets, talking of inconsequential matters.

The seventh Spell expended itself and the eighth commenced. With it the Great Hall began to empty. Slowly, the tables became less crowded, the heat diminished, and the haze became less dense.

Ronin sat with legs outstretched, swirling the dark dregs of wine in the earthenware goblet, watching the twisting reflections on its opaque surface. The general din of conversation had slackened and the clatter of the Servers clearing the tables could be heard. They hurried along the narrow aisles, huge trays filled now with the remnants of Sehna held high above their heads, out of the way of passing Bladesmen. Ronin was asked if he wished more wine and he shook his head.

He itched to leave but felt the necessity of anonymity: he did not want to depart too soon. It was possible that no one was watching, but in any event he did not want to give the impression that he had somewhere specific to be off to.

Then he saw Nirren approaching and was suddenly glad that he had stayed this long. The Chondrin sat down close to him, pouring himself a drink from the last of the wine still on the table. He smiled and looked about them. There was no one near and plenty of background noise. Still smiling, he said softly, "I think you will be interested in this. That Teck of the Magic Man's. Maastad? You remember? He works for Freidal."

Ronin put down his goblet. "A daggam?"

Nirren sipped his wine slowly, did not look directly at Ronin. "No. A teck, all right. But affiliated with Security. They do it all the time. When they are interested in something or someone, it is sometimes the only way in." He paused while a Server picked up the empty flagon. "They tried to affiliate Borros a while ago but he refused. So they sent the Rodent in to learn what he could."

"Apparently it was not enough."

"Uhm hmm. Listen, I have been given a special assignment. I have to find a Rodent of my own. I cannot tell you more now, but"—he looked at Ronin, a momentary flicker, and then his eyes were again roaming the Great Hall—"I may need your help soon, even though you may be reluctant to give it. As for the other matter—" He smiled and said in a louder voice, "Later.'"

Ronin watched his back as he departed and was lost finally in the vast sea of moving bodies.

A SOFT snore passed from his open mouth. He lay sprawled on the couch, his legs crossed at the ankles, his arms embracing a pile of tablets. His seamed face was drawn, and pouches of gray skin hung under his eyes. Even in sleep he looks tired, thought Ronin.

He crossed the room, gently shook Stahlig's shoulder. Immediately the eyes flew open, bloodshot but alert. He pulled himself up, heedless of the tumbling tablets, and cleared his throat. "Uhm, just resting for a moment."

Ronin turned, hunted for the wine. "You look like you have lost a lot of sleep."

"Just"—Stahlig pointed—"over there behind those tablets." Ronin poured the wine and he drank gratefully. "Mm, it's that overload from Downshaft, Frost take it!" His eyes shifted about the room. "A fine state when there are not enough Medicine Men in the Freehold. We may have to start using promising Students like K'reen." He finally saw the tablets on the floor. "Well." He cleared his throat again.

Flicker.

Down the Corridor and around a turning, very still and silent and watchful, they were caught in the periphery of his vision like rodents in a web.

Flicker: dark shadows against the light.

And he did not stop: he moved neither faster nor slower because they had not seen him and he did not want to do anything to attract their attention. Stillness within the organism, not without. Into the darkened surgery as fluid rolls within a jar. Now pause, let eyes adjust, and move again only when all the shadows are in their proper place. Because two daggam stand guard just down the Corridor.

"I shall take you to Borros." Stahlig drained his cup and stood.

He has not mentioned them, Ronin thought, as they went across the room and into the surgery, aware that Stahlig did not light a light or make a sound.

They stopped at the far wall and the Medicine Man reached out and touched something in the gloom. An opening appeared in the wall, automatic and perfectly silent, and they stepped into the small cubicle beyond.

It was dimly lit by two lamps, flames flickering in the draught created by the opening. Cabinets lined one side wall, a door cut into the center of the other. And Ronin had it, the pieces fitting all at once: the daggam, Stahlig's silence, the hidden door. And he looked to the far wall, at the two narrow beds, knew one was filled even before his eyes registered it, knew too that it contained a man with yellow skin, the nexus of an obscure power struggle within the Freehold.

Stahlig's arm waved like a flag. "Behold," he whispered. "Borros."

"How did you manage it?"

The Medicine Man's eyes lowered. "It was not—uhm—all that difficult. Borros had not regained consciousness when I returned the last Cycle, and I told Freidal that if he was not brought here immediately he would never again be conscious. Freidal had no choice, really."

"Would Borros have died?"

Stahlig rubbed his eyes. "Perhaps. But the important thing is that he has since awakened and talked to me." He sank onto the empty bed. "I have not yet told Freidal because I do not understand any of this. What can his value be to Freidal now? He is quite mad. Perhaps at one time—" He shook his head, and Ronin crossed the room, stood over Borros. "Such a terrible waste," Stahlig said wearily. "Human life means nothing to them. They had him for much too long—his mind is not the same."

But he did not tell them what they wanted to know, thought Ronin, or Freidal would not care whether he lives or dies now. He must have been a strong man. "Still I would talk with him," Ronin said.

Stahlig shrugged. "You can learn nothing from him. He is so full of drugs—"

Ronin turned. "Then how can you tell that he is mad?"

"It is not—"

The sound was tiny but distinct, coming from the anteroom. Stahlig jumped up, his face pale, his eyes wide. "Oh, Frost," he whispered hoarsely, "this was a mistake. I never should have agreed to it. Do not move." He passed through the doorway to the surgery, and it closed silently behind him.

Ronin stared down at Borros, at the high gleaming pate the color of old bones, at the long closed eyelids. His breathing was deeper.

The stillness was palpable. Outside he heard the low murmuring of voices. He bent over Borros, gripped the sides of his jaw in his hand. The skin felt smooth and dry. The eyelids fluttered, opened slowly, gazed blankly up at him with unfocused pupils. Still, the eyes were so extraordinary that Ronin almost failed to react to the sound behind him.

He straightened and whirled in time to see Stahlig stepping through the doorway. "Freidal wants to see me immediately," he whispered. "Probably concerned about Borros," he added needlessly. "Remain here until I have left with the messenger. I have reminded the daggam outside that their presence in here would be harmful to the patient's health. But even so, you must leave as quickly as possible. Borros has not awakened?"

"No."

"Good. Better for him to rest. And there is nothing he can tell you. You would be wasting your time." He turned to go. "Remember, as soon as you hear us leave—" He went through the doorway and disappeared into the shadows of the surgery.

Gray they were. But light gray, with golden flecks swimming in their depths like chips of bright metal. The muffled tramp of boots against concrete, diminishing. And then only the soft silence enshrouded them, with its fine susurration of breathing. The world reversed: the figures immobile, the pale flames of the lamps licking at the moving shadows they created. Still the eyes held him.

And then as if through a force of will Ronin moved silently to the closed door to the surgery, put his ear to the cool metal. He could hear nothing moving out there. He returned to the Magic Man, sat on the adjacent bed, elbows on knees. He was aware of the other door, across from him, beyond which the daggam stood guard.

"Borros," he said quietly. "Borros, can you hear me?"

There was only the sound of his breathing, lips slightly parted. His eyes stared at the ceiling, seeing nothing.

Ronin repeated the question.

Silence. No movement of the pupils.

Repeat the question: closer, louder, more insistent.

Silent but: eye movement. Blink.

Lips trembling.

"What? What did you say?"

He had to repeat it.

"So blue—"

He had to strain to hear, and thought: No sense, but contact. Repeat.

"Impossible blue. I—know it is there, I—"

Eyes focused now, golden flecks glinting. Breathing rapid. Ronin felt himself sweating, glanced quickly at the door to the Corridor. Had he heard a movement? He wiped his forehead with the back of his wrist, turned back quickly. Too late to get out now. "Borros, what are you saying?"

"An arch—yes, it—it must look like an arch, so vast, so—" He jerked as Ronin touched him, head whipping around, eyes bulging. His lips drew back in a laugh that was more an animal snarl, bared teeth gleaming. "Ahahaha! But there is nothing there, you have nothing no notes and now no more head brain squeezed until it's dry and that's what it is dry so it's no use why don't you st—" His eyes drooped momentarily, then the lids flew up and he stared as if just coming awake. "No—no more I"—shake of the head—"do what you want, all usel—ugh!"—he shivered down the length of his body—"the land brown and rich and plants growing green and free with no tanks and the heat of the bare sun hang—hanging in all that space!"

He stopped there like a mechanism run down and incapable of beginning again. And Ronin thought: It's no good this way, no good at all. He *does* sound like a madman. His words are clear but they have no meaning. He wiped away more sweat, knowing that there was very little time.

Missed something, he thought. But what? Think.

He leaned forward, said urgently: "The land, Borros, tell me more about the land." The Magic Man had thought Ronin was one of the Security interrogators. So his approach had been wrong. Get into his mind: what if he was not mad? Only thing to try.

And he saw Borros's mouth working. "Yes, the land." The faintest whisper like a dry wind, and Ronin felt a surge of adrenaline. "The fields, food to eat, great flowing waters, new life for the people but—" He gasped as if struck by a blow, and Ronin reached out to hold him.

The long eyes were deep pools where golden fish swam frenziedly. "Oh, Frost, no! Not again!" Eyes popping, face very pale, white lines netting the sides of the mouth, a living skull. As if staring into the face of Death—or a being more terrible.

He strained to sit up but Ronin held him down as gently as he could, feeling the flight of forces within the thin frame. "Must, must!" Beads of sweat clung to the tight yellow skin of his head. It gathered on his upper lip, ran into his mouth, and the tongue came out, licked at the moisture. Sweat dripped along the sides of Ronin's face as he stared at the twisting, tortured countenance. It rolled along his wrists and onto the backs of his hands, seeping between his fingers, and he tightened his grip. Borros's hands were like claws, the tendons corded and raised just beneath the skin, held out in front of him as if warding off his agony and terror. Then he seized Ronin's arms.

They were locked, immobile, and Ronin, caught in the pull of the gray-and-gold eyes, felt that he had lost volition of independent movement.

"It is coming!"

Bound within the moment, he felt the writhings of Borros's mind—

"I have seen—It—"

—knew with an awful certainty suddenly flooding his being that Something was there—

"—draws closer—the people cannot st—"

—not a presence but merely the threat of a presence, and that was enough to—

"Must go to them—help—hel—"

"Who, Borros, who? We are the only—"

The jaws snapped closed, the eyes saw him, perhaps for the first time, and the terrible ivory grin came again and now Ronin felt as if he faced—what?

"Fool!" hissed Borros. "They want no one to know.

A secret!" And he laughed without humor. "*Their* secret!" The eyes took on a glossy depth, the pupils
huge. Veins stood out along his temples where the
Dehn spots pulsed as if alive. "Fool! We are not alone
on this world!" Eyes bulging alarmingly, teeth grinding
in effort. "But it—will mean nothing. It comes—
comes to destroy everything. Unless—" His head
whipped from side to side, with a spray of sweat. His
throat convulsed and it appeared that he cried out, although the sound was low and strangled and seemed
barely human. "Death—death is coming!"

Borros jerked again and went limp, his eyes fluttering closed. Ronin let go of him then, his hands and
arms numb. He put his ear to Borros's chest, then
quickly pushed rhythmically with his palms. He listened again. Pounded his fist once, twice, over the
heart. Listened again.

He wiped his dripping face and stood up. Moving to
the doorway to the surgery, he pressed a part of the
wall and darkness bloomed before him. He stepped
through, out of the light. The door closed. He listened
for a moment. His eyes adjusted. All shadows in their
place. Then, like Stahlig before him, he disappeared
into the shadows.

"WHAT do you know of the Magic Men!"

"What brought that to mind?"

"You are always answering a question with another question—Oh yes! There." The hand moved, flesh on flesh, orange and light brown in the low guttering lamplight. Black pooled in the hollows.

"Just a peculiar topic to bring up now," Ronin said softly.

K'reen moved slowly, gently against him. Cascading dark hair, soft and cool, accentuating the heat of their bodies. "Not at all. They are purported to be—oh!— the saviors of the Freehold, divining ways for us to live in case the Great Machines cease to function. Is that not true?"

Hands moving from orange to black, light to shadow. "So it is said." Their lips met and opened.

K'reen licked the side of his neck. "With all the political talk going on—the rumors of the Saardin— mmm—it's natural to be thinking of the future."

"I know very little of them," he whispered. But the temptation was very strong within him.

She rolled away from him, the lamplight licking at the indentation of her spine, the crease of her buttocks. "Won't you ever talk to me?" she said in a small voice.

"There is nothing to talk about." He reached out and she drew away.

"You mean you have nothing to say to me."

Ronin sat up in the bed and stared at the dark bell of her hair sweeping across the pillows. "That is not at all what I meant."

She turned on him, eyes flashing. "But it is!" she cried.

"You are twisting what I say. Why do you do that?"

"I will not play this game."

"There is no game." There was an edge to his voice now.

"I will not let you turn this back on me. You're the one who—"

"K'reen, this is not the time—"

"Not the time?" She sat up too. "You must be joking! There is nothing more important for us to do."

"Yes, there is," he said sharply.

She glared at him for an instant and he felt the charge build within her. She lunged, her open palm striking him across the face with considerable force. "Chill take you!" she hissed.

He caught her extended arm at the wrist, pulled it forward and down with some violence so that she was suddenly on her back beneath him. He lowered himself. The soft light gleamed off the whites of her eyes. Her breasts heaved under him, the nipples hard, and she brought her knee up into his hip on the edge of the pelvic bone, but he pressed the nerve on the inside of her thigh, numbing it. "Frost!" she breathed, and pulled his head down to hers, arching her body against him, thighs open.

He made love with a strange kind of desperation, trying, in his confusion and anguish, to lose his mind in his body. And so involved was he in this that he failed to notice a similar despair in K'reen.

He rolled away from her sleeping form, sat on the edge of the bed, and lit the lamp. Its pale flame sent the darkness skittering away in all directions. He kept the light low so as not to wake her. He heard nothing but the white noise of silence in his ears as he stared into the flame and saw again the dream from which he had awakened. . . .

He is in the Freehold, yet it is of a different construction from that of the real Freehold. It is under the earth but it is a City, with massive structures that rise through the air to such heights that they almost touch the rock vault above. Dreamscape: suprareal.

He is in one such structure, high up, with K'reen. They are preparing to leave; he cannot think where they are going to. Suddenly the structure trembles heavily. Cracks appear in the walls, and he feels the rumbling in his bones. He looks outside. Structures all around are coming apart and collapsing as the earth continues to heave and split. He hears screaming and sees the red belch of columns of flame.

He cannot find K'reen. He runs out into the Corridor and is met with the choke of smoke and falling rubble; the structure is tearing itself apart. He calls her name. Over and over. He hears echoes, echoes only.

He runs then down the Stairwell, fearing at any moment it will collapse under him.

He reaches the Outside at last and finds—He is in a cool glade of green foliage, dark and moist. A rich, unfamiliar scent comes to him from the earth. His face is wet. And his arms. Drops of water from above hit him all over. Across a river he sees the Freehold disassemble itself and come crashing down amidst huge fires. Bright sparks twist in the air. But he is not there and he wonders at this as he opens his eyes and finds that he is lying beside K'reen in the dark. . . .

He sighed now, once, a long inhalation and exhalation of breath, to help rid himself of the last strands of the dream. It had been very vivid. He lay back in bed, put a pillow behind his back, and thought about Borros. For half the length of a Spell he replayed over and over in his mind what the Magic Man had said.

And at the end of that time he thought that perhaps his dream had not after all been dispelled.

TIME, Ronin decided, to see the Salamander.

In the Sector the Lift was out, its sliding doors frozen irretrievably half open. Deep parallel lines were scored down one door, as if some large and angry animal had been frustrated by its stasis. The other one was crumpled like an old Bladesman's Combat wound. So he took to the Stairwell and, on the way Upshaft, had time to recall his first meeting with the Salamander.

Combat had always been a game to him. Like every other element in his young life, it was too inconsequential to be taken seriously. On what had come to be known as the Combat Level, the normal Freehold cubicles had, some time before, been scooped out and replaced by a series of large indoor courtyards that now served as training grounds for Combat. Each Cycle at his allotted time, he would file into the Hall of Combat, the largest of these courtyards, along with other Students of his age. Half a Spell of strenuous exercise would eventually give way to a lecture on the art of killing and maiming through ritual moves, after which the Students would be paired off for actual practice.

He had never given much thought to the art one way or another, he was a Student because he had been told to be a Student, therefore he was at best mediocre. Often his mind would wander and his opponent would easily disarm him. This never appeared to bother him, but for the Instructor it was a different matter entirely. Ronin's indifference infuriated him, and it would not be uncommon for the Student to bear the brunt of his wrath in front of the assembled Class.

During one practice, Ronin observed a heavy man, almost gross-looking, stride easily into the Hall. "Students," called the Instructor, and the sounds of iron striking iron ceased immediately. He turned to the newcomer, and with a flourish of his hand introduced him. "Students, the Salamander." There was a buzz of excited whispering amongst the boys, which the Instructor contrived to ignore. "As you know—" He waited impatiently for silence. "As you know, the Salamander is the Sensii of Arms of the Freehold. He is here to observe your progress." There was more whispering, and the Instructor was forced to cover another pause by clearing his throat. He looked sternly around the Hall. "*Some* of you may be lucky enough to be chosen to study with the Salamander himself."

Ronin was aware of the undercurrent of envy that ran now through the Instructor's voice, and he turned to look at the Salamander, but his face, with its heavy jowls, oddly high cheekbones and glossy black eyes, remained impassive. At this moment, the Salamander raised one hand, encrusted with flashing jewels, and in a rich, slightly nasal voice said, "Pray continue your practicing, boys; do let me see what you are made of."

"Come, come, Students," called the Instructor nervously, clapping his hands, "on with it now." Almost as one, they turned each to his partner, and once again the walls rang with the clash of metal.

Out of the corner of his eye, Ronin tried as best he could to keep the Salamander in sight as he commenced his round of the Hall, the Instructor a pace behind him.

"Listen, you," growled his practice partner, a huge, brutish Student of mean temperament, "it was just my ill fortune to be paired with you this Cycle." He grunted as he swung his sword in a vicious arc at Ronin's stomach. Ronin stepped back, took the brunt of the blow on the edge of his own blade, the force turning it, and there was a sharp scraping sound. A shiver raced up his arm and his fingers went momentarily numb.

"But you will give me a good fight," the Student said menacingly, "when the Salamander comes our way. I have been waiting—unngh!" he grunted again as he swung, "for this chance for a long time."

Ronin, who had been thinking also of the Salamander, said, "Korlik, is that his real name?"

Korlik snorted, as close to a laugh as he could come. "Fool!—ungh!—no one knows." The blade came whistling at him once again. "Why don't you ask him—unngh!—when he passes by?" Ronin continued to defend himself against Korlik's pressing attack.

"Haw!—ungh!—I will tell why you won't —unngh!—because you are going to be flat on your back, looking at the bottom—ungh!—of my boot.

I mean for him to see me and—uhnn!—take me Up-shaft. Understand?"

But Ronin's attention was focused on the approaching figure of the Salamander; only part of himself was given over to the automatic defense of his person. The Sensii was a mountain of flesh garbed in cloth of jet and crimson. How much was muscle, he wondered. And what of his reflexes? His weight must be enormous. Still, he was Sensii. The Master of Combat.

Korlik growled at him. "He is coming this way. Chill take you, have you heard what I said?—ungh! Put on a good show, Ronin, I'm warning you—uhnn!"

The two figures were almost abreast of them as Ronin turned his full attention to the Combat. "Show?" he said. "There will be no show. Not for you, not for the Salamander."

Cursing, Korlik bore down upon him and, seeing the Salamander and the Instructor reach them, began to hammer Ronin with blows.

"Now this one, Sensii," said the Instructor obsequiously, "is Korlik. Big and strong and he shows fine potential. Unfortunately, he is paired this practice with an inferior Stu—"

"Pray cease," said the Salamander, lifting a jeweled hand, "your useless chatter. Do not presume to make judgements for me." Ronin was pleased to see the Instructor's eyes bulge in his narrow face and his tongue working in his open mouth as he fought to control himself.

During this time Korlik had not lessened his attack upon Ronin, who neither put up a concerted defense in any of the prescribed ways nor counterattacked. He preferred to move, using his own blade only when absolutely necessary to turn aside his opponent's sword.

The Instructor, seeing potential disaster for himself in Ronin's refusal to conform to the lessons, made noises for the Salamander to move on. But the Sensii graced him with a momentary glance, frosty and disdainful, and he was silenced.

"Boys," the Salamander said, "desist for the moment." Korlik, sweat rolling down his arms, soaking his shirt, dropped his sword with great reluctance and glowered at Ronin.

The Salamander stroked the end of his long nose between thumb and forefinger, his dark eyes fixed on Ronin. "And what is your name, dear boy?"

"Ronin."

"Ronin, *sir*," corrected the Instructor.

The Salmander's eyes rolled up briefly toward the ceiling. "Kindly be good enough to take your person across the Hall so that I will not be obliged to suffer your presence." He said it with a sighing exhalation of breath, not at all forcefully, Ronin thought. Nevertheless, the Instructor stalked off without another word, the muscles at the sides of his jaw working spasmodically.

Around them, the din of practice continued unabated, crashing off the walls and echoing back upon the ear. The acrid stench of sweat and fear hung in the vast Hall, staining the air.

"Sensii," said Korlik. "I have waited for this time, working long and hard in the hope that I would please you. It is my greatest wish to be taught by you."

The eyes of the Salamander, black and hard as chips of stone, turned upon Korlik. "My boy," he drawled, "only the most *special* Students, those who exhibit extraordinary merit, work with me." The eyes flicked up and down his body. "Rest assured that you are not one of those. Now pray be still." Korlik strangled a gasp and ground his teeth in fury, but he remained silent.

The Salamander turned to Ronin and said as if they were in a room alone, "Tell me why you do Combat in such a manner."

He wondered what the Salamander wanted; wondered what sort of answer would be best to give. In the end, he told the truth. "Combat bores me," he said evenly.

"Then why do you bother with it?"

"I do it because I have to."

The Salamander rubbed his nose again, the rings on his fingers catching the light. "Hmm, yes, I suppose you do." Abruptly he said: "You think of other matters."

"Sir?" He was startled.

"When you do Combat," the Salamander expounded patiently, as if explaining an obvious fact to a child, "your mind is thinking of other things."

"Why, yes," he replied, somewhat surprised. "Yes, my mind is often elsewhere when I fight."

"Please." A pained expression muddied his features momentarily. "To do Combat is *not* to 'fight,' dear boy. 'Fighting' is done by animals. Combat is a ritualistic art performed by civilized men."

"I never gave it much thought," Ronin said snidely. Because he was growing interested in spite of himself and this perplexed him.

The Salamander was not at all ruffled. "Ah well, motivation is everything, dear boy. You have natural ability, as any halfwit can see. But motivation—ah!—

now that is another matter entirely. What can we do to elicit your interest, hmm? We shall have to attend to that." So saying, he retreated a pace. His long sword hung at his side, encased in its ornate jet-and-scarlet-lacquered scabbard. "Yes, we must work on that. Defend yourself, dear boy."

His hand went not to the hilt of his sword but to the folds of his wide scarlet sash, producing a burnished-metal fan. Ronin could not believe his eyes, but still he put up his sword. The fan wove complex patterns in the air, opening and closing.

The Salamander's attack was over almost before it had commenced, or so it seemed to Ronin. At its swift completion, he was left weaponless, the extended top edge of the fan a bright arc at his throat.

"Hawhawhaw!" Korlik bellowed at his humiliation, but Ronin's thoughts were elsewhere, on the fan's mysterious dances.

Observing the inwardness of Ronin's colorless eyes, the Salamander smiled slightly. He folded the fan and replaced it within his sash. "Report to my Level in three Cycles' time," he said briskly. "Do not bring any personal items."

He turned on his heel and strode powerfully across the crowded Hall to advise the Instructor of the Students he had chosen, and disappeared down the Corridor in a swirl of jet and crimson, like some elegant and untouchable bird.

He reached the cool Corridor without passing anyone; visitors were rare this far Upshaft. The tan walls arched away from him clean and empty. Here the usual cement floor had been covered in resilient wood planking, enameled a rich deep brown.

As he walked, the walls lightened until they reached a cream color, and he stopped in front of huge double doors with thickly carved panels along their edges. Heavy metal knockers in the likeness of a thin twisting lizard, needle tongue exposed, flames writhing at its feet, were hung in the center of each door. Tiny ruby eyes glinted in the strong light of the Overheads. He stood in front of the doors and did not touch the knockers.

"Yes?" a flat filtered voice said from nowhere.

He did not stir: he knew the routine. He pronounced his name clearly.

There was nothing for a moment, then the disembodied voice said: "Former Student?"

"Yes."

A crackle. A brief hum.

"Enter," the voice said.

It was large and gave the appearance of being light and airy and open without actually being so; no room in the Freehold could, by definition.

The deliberately rough-finished walls were painted a light blue, the ceiling a soft white. The planking on the floor was lacquered a deep, lustrous blue. Low chairs were scattered about the front part of the room. The walls were devoid of any ornamentation. Double doors, the twins of the ones he had just come through, broke up the far wall.

He went across the room and stood in front of a desk that appeared to be very old. Behind it sat a woman with light, wavy hair, and a face broad and flat enough to make it interesting. She wore a robe the same color as the walls.

He looked into her disinterested gray eyes.

"You wished—?" The cool question hung in the air like a beaded curtain.

"To see the Salamander," he said.

"Ah." She said it as if it were a word with meaning. She gazed at him and let the silence stretch itself like a yawn. Her small neat hands fluttered over the desktop, the lacquered nails glistening in the light.

Eventually she said, "I am afraid he is unavailable at the moment." There was no trace of regret in her voice.

"Just give him my name, please."

"Perhaps if you returned during a later Spell."

"Have you given him my name? Have you told him that I am here?"

The nails scratched their way along the wood. "He is extremely busy and—"

He leaned over, captured her hands in his, pressed them down. She stared at them as if fascinated, and raised her eyes to his.

"Tell him," he said softly.

"Still—" She continued to look at him, searching his face. Her tongue showed briefly between her white teeth like a coral snake.

He released her and she got up and went out through the doors behind her. She left a soft humming and a breeze wafting from a sudden source. Borne upon it was a gentle hint of cloves, and if he had not spent so much time on this Level, he would have supposed that it came from the woman.

She took her time coming back and when she

emerged her gray eyes were round, as if she were a bit startled. She held one door open.

"You may go in now," she said a little breathlessly.

Ronin smiled to himself and, as he passed her, he saw something moving in her eyes, an ambiguous emotion. She stared after him.

"The last door on the right," she called as if it were an afterthought.

The hallway was painted the lightest blue imaginable over the same rough-textured base. The floor repeated the dark blue. He passed doors on either side at regular intervals.

It ended in a blank wall. Doors to right and left. He rapped with his knuckles. It opened.

The odor of cloves was sharper now. A young man stood in the doorway so that Ronin could see beyond him. He wore close-fitting breeches and a shirt of a soft tan color and short dark gleaming boots. He was slim and had unnaturally red cheeks, as if he had just spent a full Spell scrubbing his face. His lips were full and pink. His short, curly, blond hair shone. Over his heart he wore a jewel-hilted dagger in a scabbard of blood-red leather; another rode on his right hip. He had the appearance of never having done anything in his life.

He stared hard at Ronin and his lips parted slightly. They remained that way for a long moment and then, abruptly, he stood aside and Ronin entered.

It was darker than in the hallway and it took him a moment to adjust. He was in a huge room, paneled in wood. Thick carpets of dark, swirling patterns covered the floor. One wall was lined from floor to ceiling with books. Functional leather chairs were grouped casually. A long plush couch was set against one half of the back wall. Open double doors with separate iron-grillwork gates took up the other half. The sounds of water flowing came to him and the scent of cloves came heavily to his nostrils.

There were many men in the room, all dressed, as far as Ronin could tell in the uncertain light, similarly to the man with the red cheeks. They contrived to ignore him with an affected languor.

"Drink?" the red-cheeked man asked, and when Ronin shook his head, he drifted off, looking rather pleased.

Ronin was very interested in the wall of books and he went over to look at them. He ran his fingertips along the rows of spines and thought of G'fand. They were all extremely old, of course, with worn leather bindings. Some, he saw, had required repairs. He opened one at random. The characters were unfamiliar and he tried another Glyphs: still unreadable. Ah, G'fand, how you would revel in this: an entire world for you. Books! And all they had Downshaft were fragments. A sudden sadness gripped him.

The red-cheeked man beckoned to him, stretched his arm toward the doorway in the far wall. Ronin passed him. He put a delicate forefinger to his lower lip.

It looked to be an open patio, but that was impossible. Even so, it was a square room whose very high ceiling and diffused lighting gave it a tremendously open feeling. He went across the stone flagging while a breeze stirred his hair. Quite suddenly, he was curious.

All of this was a part of the Salamander's quarters that he had not seen before.

He heard strange sounds: a small high trilling, a repeated whistling, others he could not isolate. They seemed to emanate from high up in the air.

He passed, in the center of the room, a square pool of water, which bubbled and gurgled, fed from some hidden source.

On the far side of the pool, some distance away, was the Salamander. He sat on a bare wooden chair with thick arms. A small stone table with crystal flagon and goblets was on his left side. A second chair stood near, empty and waiting.

He was wearing a dull black robe under which he wore jet leggings and a loose shirt. His high black boots were polished to a gloss. A scarlet sash banded his ample waist. Just below his throat, like a startling splash of fresh blood, lay an uncurling lizard carved from a single ruby, its body graceful and rich in color, slightly translucent. Its eyes were of jet, and onyx flames danced around it, arching up into its mouth.

He looked not a moment older than the day Ronin had first met him. Large, squarish face with highly pronounced cheekbones that, had he not heavy jowls, would have given him almost an alien cast. Thick, black brows shielded deep-set eyes as jet-black and shiny-hard as those on his brooch. His hair was thick and dark and long, brushed back away from his high forehead to give the impression of small wings.

"My dear, dear boy!" the Salamander exclaimed from his chair. "How pleasing it is to see you again after all this time!" He smiled his jowly smile, the skin at the corners of his eyes crinkling.

Ronin gazed into the onyx eyes and was not fooled. They were heavy-lidded, the lashes long, but he knew what lay behind that effete exterior.

"Come, come. Do sit down beside me." With a diffident wave of his thickly ringed fingers he indicated the empty chair. Ronin went up two wide flat steps and sat.

The Salamander reached over to the crystal flagon, but Ronin declined.

"And what do you think of my atrium?" asked the Salamander.

Ronin looked around, said blandly, "Is that what it is?"

The Salamander laughed deep in his throat; the corners of his eyes crinkled and he showed his white even teeth. But the eyes remained unchanged. "Many centuries ago, when people lived on the surface of this planet, they built houses, low, separate dwellings, you see, with a central room open to the natural elements: the sun and the rain and the stars, and there they gathered to relax and talk of pleasant matters and smell the fresh air. A marvelous custom, do you not agree?"

He changed tones abruptly. "My dear Ronin, I have told you a thousand times that you must be more well read."

"If I may say so, it is quite out of the question without access to a library such as yours. Books are a rarity Downshaft."

At that moment the red-cheeked man stepped through the far doorway and the Salamander looked over. "You have met Voss, my Chondrin." It was not a question.

"He seems quite attracted to doors," Ronin said.

The Salamander shifted minutely in his chair; the jet eyes were unblinking. "Dear boy," he said without inflection, "one of these times you will make a remark like that to a person without a sense of humor—a person with power—and then you will be in most serious trouble. Voss can do a great many things very well indeed."

He gestured and the Chondrin dropped to a crouch. Both hands became a blur and Ronin was aware of an angry humming cutting through the background sounds. The brickwork of the wall to the left and behind him crackled and he turned to look. Two very deep incisions had been cut barely a centimeter apart. On the stone floor directly below lay the two jewel-hilted daggers that had, up to a moment before, been sheathed at Voss's heart and hip. A split second was all that he had needed to throw both with deadly accuracy.

Ronin turned back to the Salamander.

"He has no sense of humor."

Again the big man's deep laugh echoed off the walls. "You always had peculiar ways of letting me know the people you disapproved of." He rubbed his nose. "Which was almost everyone, I might add." With a flick of his fingers he dismissed the Chondrin, who, after retrieving his weapons, withdrew, closing the gates after him.

The Salamander breathed deeply. "Ah! Feel that! It is almost like being on the surface three centuries ago. Do you hear the birds? Did you recognize the calls? You are sufficiently knowledgeable to have heard of birds." He waved, a curiously brusque movement for such a normally expansive gesture. "All of this is not wasted on you, I trust," he drawled.

Ronin forced himself to sit completely still and say nothing.

The Salamander's right arm, lying thickly along the arm of his chair, was somehow menacing. "Let me tell you something. It has been many years since you have been here. Everything has changed."

He cocked his head to one side as if listening to a far-off but important conversation. "How peaceful it is here," he said after a time, his tone soft and reflective. "How comfortable, how secure. It took me quite a long time to build all this. For instance, this room was under construction when you were last here. It has taken an enormous effort to get all the elements gathered and integrated. The lighting was difficult but, as you can see, not insurmountable. But the birds, the birds, dear boy! For a while I thought I would never hear them in here." He cocked his head again. Their sweet singing sounded over the music of the water. "Ah, listen! In the end it was worth it. This place gives me great pleasure."

There was silence for a time, at least a cessation of human speech, during which a kind of dreamy peacefulness descended upon them.

Broken. "And you have changed the most, dear boy. You are no longer my Student. You are a Bladesman. That is in itself significant."

Ronin let out the breath he had been holding. "Yes?"

"It means that you have been extremely fortunate in not having run across a Saardin without a sense of humor." Once more he laughed. Ronin thought he liked to hear the sound of it.

The laughter died suddenly. "Or have you? One hears the most distressing stories. You seem to have put yourself into a somewhat embarrassing position." One eyebrow arched, giving him a vividly predatory look.

"What have you been told?"

He shifted his bulk in the chair. "Enough to wonder how much of your training here you still remember. Freidal distrusts you, that is not a good thing." He looked down at his jeweled hand, then up again. "He can become quite—um—annoying."

Ronin sat rather stiffly. "I did not come to you for that reason."

"Indeed? But I daresay that you will have to adjust to the fact that you blundered. He has marked you; perhaps he is having you watched. I need only—"

"No."

"I thought not. It makes no sense, but then—" He shrugged. "Perhaps then you will tell me why you came."

Ronin nodded. "It is about a Magic Man," he said.

For a time after he had finished, the Salamander said nothing. He laced his fingers, resting them on his thighs. The scent of cloves came very strong on the air. The "birds" sang. Along one wall, moss had been encouraged to grow, moist and green. Ronin found it hard to believe that they were underground. He felt isolated, quite disconnected from the world Downshaft, and he recognized this as a form of offering. It was no accident that the Salamander had received him here.

"How do you suppose," the Salamander said, "I am able to maintain all of this?" His hands unfolded like a fan.

Ronin thought: So it has been a mistake after all. He got up.

The Salamander's eyes opened wide. "Ah. What is it?"

"There was a time when this was necessary," Ronin said angrily. "Now—"

"Indulge me."

"As you said, everything has changed."

"Did I not teach you all explanations in their proper time?"

"I am no longer your student."

"You made that quite clear some time ago."

The onyx eyes were all pupil, black and glittery, locked with Ronin's. An electric charge built itself in the room.

"All right," the Salamander said finally. "All right. Sit down. Be assured that I have an answer for you. At least let me reach it at my own pace."

The gates opened across the room and Voss appeared as if by a signal. He came immediately across to them and stood in front of the Salamander, who said, "Open the Lens."

Voss shot Ronin a quick glance, then nodded and went out through a narrow door behind them that Ronin had failed to notice before.

"Now where were we?" The Salamander cocked his head. "Ah, yes, my not so humble quarters. They are extensive. When you were last here, you saw only what all my Students are allowed to see. You could have—" He shook his head. "But old ground is pointless." He rubbed his hands down the smooth wood of the arms. "I have an entire Sector, you know."

Ronin was surprised in spite of himself. "No, I did not."

He nodded. "But that is only part of it, an insignificant part. Decoration, one might say. One impresses those who must be impressed. For the rest, it is all pleasure. And it is only the tip, having it. Getting it, that is what counts. To do that, one needs but one item: Power." He leaned forward. "I have it."

"So it is said."

The onyx eyes bored into him.

"You do not fear it," the Salamander said, not without some contempt. "That is a mistake."

"I do not worship it."

"You would do well to heed me."

"That time—"

"Yes, quite." The Salamander rose gracefully. "If you will follow me."

He crossed to the narrow door and led Ronin into darkness.

Light that bloomed in front of him was dim and faded, the colors smeary and washed out, as if, having been painted quickly and tentatively on canvas, they were now covered in a fine film of dust.

He saw himself as a small child, and everything looked too large for him to use. He was in a room filled with stifled silence. It was very hot and he pulled at the collar of his shirt. It seemed he could not breathe. He wished his sister were here. She was very young, her features still forming, but he loved her. She would come to him when she was sad or lonely or had

had a fight, and he would comfort her, help her, protect her. And then she would laugh and hug him around the waist and her happiness would transmit itself to him. She could make him smile. Why isn't she here, why are all these people here, what's wrong? Someone said: "It is no use, they have called it off." A figure loomed over him. What's wrong, what's wrong? The figure said: "Your sister is dead. Can you understand that? Dead." He began to cry. The figure slapped him hard. Someone said: "He is too young." The figure hit him again and again until he stopped.

"—in this room." It was small, lit only by points of glowing green light, winking like jewels from some far-off city. Ronin rubbed briefly at his eyes.

"Very few people have been in this room," the Salamander continued. "Very few people even know of its existence." Voss was sitting before a metal box, low and wide, from the center of which an oval cylinder projected perhaps a meter into the air. His hands were busy moving across a complex control panel. "Do you follow me?" The Salamander moved behind Voss, put a jeweled hand on his shoulder. "I think that you were wise to stay awhile longer."

He turned and the tiny jet eyes at his throat flashed, reflecting flatly the hard green light. The lizard's body had taken on a dull, dusky hue, like the film on stagnant water. "This Magic Man, is he sane or mad? You are unsure."

He lifted his arm, the palm of his hand standing out dead white against the dense black of his robes—even the scarlet sash was turned black by the strange light. "This is the Lens. We do not know how it works, or even its original purpose, but in a moment you shall see what few men in our lifetime have ever seen. Look. Look upward." And he squeezed Voss's shoulder.

At first Ronin thought that the ceiling had in some way opened. A swirling opalescent oval lit the darkness. Then he saw that it was a projection from the cylinder of the Lens.

Pearl grays and the lightest of violets swam blurrily above them. Then quite suddenly the scene was sharply delineated. And Ronin stared in awe. This cannot be, he thought. How is it possible?

Thick banks of magenta cloud and pearled, frigid mist whipped by them, forming, and then were gone. The light was diffuse and cold. It seemed infinite.

"Yes," said the Salamander softly and dramatically, "we are indeed observing the sky above our planet. This is the outer shell of the world, Ronin."

Slowly the layers moved upward and out of their field of view as the Lens shifted its focus. They became lighter, finer, shredding before their eyes like gossamer robes.

"We shall now take a look at the surface of the world."

A whiteness, a terrible frosty barrenness. Sheets of snow and ice picked up by the heavy winds, dragged across the frozen mountains and crevasses, raking the terrain. Ice and snow and rock and not a hint of anything else. It was impossible for anything to live Up there.

"This is the world," the Salamander intoned. "Destroyed by the Ancients. Devastated beyond any hope of redemption. A desolate, decaying hulk, useless now. You are seeing what is directly above us, Ronin.

This is why we remain encased three kilometers below the surface. To reach the surface is to die. No food, no shelter, no warmth, no one."

"But is it all this way?" asked Ronin. "The Magic Man spoke of a land where the ground was brown and green plants grew."

The Salamander's rings glinted as he squeezed Voss' shoulder again. The scene above them dissolved, shifted, yet all was the same. Ice and snow.

"The range of the Lens is finite. However, for our purposes here, it is more than enough. What you see now is over fifty kilometers distance. And now—" Dissolve. "One hundred and fifty kilometers distant." Dissolve. "More than five hundred kilometers away. As you can see, it is all the same. Nothing lives in the world, save us. We are the last. The other Freeholds are gone, contact lost many centuries ago. The Magic Man is quite mad. Perhaps his mind snapped from the constant pressure he was under—they are a strange breed. Or perhaps—"

Ronin turned. "What do you know?"

The Salamander smiled. "My dear boy, I know as much of this matter as you have seen fit to tell me. But I know Security. And their methods can be somewhat —ah—debilitating at times. It is all according to what Freidal wants."

"But Security has no right to—"

"Dear boy, wielding power is the only right," he said sternly, then softening: "It is all very personal, surely you have learned that by now."

He removed his hand and the window onto the bleak world above winked out. The green glow came up again.

"In any event, this Magic Man has been known for some while to be most difficult; quite a dissident, at times. But then they all are when time-allotment rolls around."

The velvet darkness enclosed them snugly. From out of it, Ronin heard the Salamander's voice, soft and reassuring. "I trust, dear boy, that this extraordinary demonstration has eliminated all your doubts."

"IT is the twenty-ninth Cycle."

He was wide-shouldered and slightly smaller than average, a fact to which, many believed, he had never quite adjusted. His hair was short and dark, coming low on his forehead, giving him a forbidding countenance which he cultivated and used to full effect. Deep lines scored downward from the corners of his ungenerous mouth even when his face was in repose.

He stood on a small raised platform, dressed in white robes, believing the color made him appear larger, and addressed his students—Bladesmen—who were arrayed before him in precise rows under the high vault of the Hall of Combat.

"This Cycle, iron strikes iron," the Instructor continued, in the prescribed manner, his head swiveling on his thin neck. "For this is the Cycle of the Arm and the Wrist and the Sword. This Cycle we are called by the Horn of Combat.

His stentorian voice took some time dying away in the vast Hall. In the silence, there was a rustling as the

Bladesmen, in perfect cadence, opened a square space in the center of the Hall. On all four sides they stood rigidly then, facing inward toward the opening, waiting.

There came a note upon the air. Both deep and shrill, it echoed off the walls, seeming to pick up overtones so that it increased in volume before ending. It came again. And a third time.

"It is the twenty-ninth Cycle," repeated the Instructor. "The Horn of Combat has been sounded. It is both a reminder and a warning. A reminder of our past, of what we must strive to preserve with our last breath. A warning to all foes present and future that we are ever vigilant in our sacred trust to guard the Freehold from all who would seek her destruction. . . ."

The words of Tradition droned on, as they had, Ronin supposed, for centuries. They were meaningless to him now. And he wondered if that had not always been so. The Salamander was correct in one matter: it *was* indeed all personal. Freidal's carefully phrased words of sacred Tradition were as much a fraud as his fabrication of the detention of the mad Magic Man. Yet Ronin was well aware that the Security Saardin's belief in Tradition was unwavering. Personal.

". . . your pledge that we shall ever remember our sacred duty to the perpetuation of the Freehold above all else." But for the soft rustle of cloth, the occasional creak of new leather, silence descended on the Hall.

The Instructor's round eyes narrowed and he thrust out his jaw as he scanned the multitude before him. He relished the power he held over the Bladesmen. This was his domain, and for as long as they were within it, they performed as he bade them. His nostrils flared and he delicately sniffed the air. Cutting through the stench of ten score bodies fresh from half a Spell's exercise, as separate, as distinct as if it were the perfume of flowers in full bloom, was the peculiar odor of fear. His nostrils dilated again as he drank in the heady smell, almost dizzying in its intensity. His mouth curled up slightly and he gripped the railing before him.

Ronin, who had been trained to observe faces in his years Upshaft, saw the Instructor's secret smile and felt as if he were spying on something unclean. His mouth curled in distaste and he thought on the complexities of power and how, however much he tried, he could not evade its sphere of influence.

"Ronin," called the Instructor. "Step into the Square of Combat."

Without surprise, Ronin moved from his position within the multitude of Bladesmen into the open Square. He turned and faced the Instructor.

"Bladesman, are you prepared to do Combat?"

"Instructor, I am."

The Instructor addressed the Class. "This Cycle, as a demonstration for you newer Bladesmen as well as the veterans, we are privileged to be allowed a Bladesman from another Class, so that you may observe other techniques and compare them with your own." He paused to allow the murmuring of the Bladesmen to subside. Ronin was completely alert now. Students generally fought within their own Classes primarily to forestall the creation of grudges that might involve the honor of Classes as a whole. Among Bladesmen, the resolution of quarrels was encouraged through individual Combat matches.

"We have a Bladesman from the eighth-Spell
Class." The Instructor raised an arm. "Marcsh, step
forward."

A thick, stolid figure now parted the throng and
made its way into the Square. He walked purposefully
with just a hint of a swagger, brushing aside Bladesmen too close to him. A smile was tacked onto his
square mouth.

Skill at ritualism, thought Ronin, and prepared
himself mentally for Combat. One of Nirren's favorite
topics was that of coincidence: he rejected the concept
completely. Ronin did not share this belief, although it
seemed an inarguable point. Yet here, at this moment,
he must side with the Chondrin. The Instructor could
not possibly have picked Marcsh by chance; it would
certainly be dangerous to think along those lines.

Marcsh's greedy, close-set eyes stared at him with
undisguised malice. Then he turned and faced the Instructor.

"Bladesman, are you prepared to do Combat?"

"Instructor, I am."

Ronin wondered what would happen if he asked the
Instructor to tell the Class who Marcsh really was. But
he did not consider actually doing it because the adrenaline was already rising within him like a great and
powerful animal. He wanted this match.

"As a Student of the eighth-Spell Class, do you
agree to be bound by my judgement in this Combat?"

Marcsh was staring again at Ronin. "I do," he said.

The Instructor gestured to a thin pale boy on his
right who stood perfectly still beside a small burnished-metal gong. He held a short mallet in his hand.

The Instructor addressed both Combatants. "You will commence when you hear the Tone. You will cease only when the Tone sounds again. Is this acknowledged?"

The Instructor gestured again and the boy swung the mallet in a shallow arc. The crystal tone hung in the air for seconds, refusing to die.

Combat had begun.

Sight, then sound, repeating. And Ronin began to retreat under the frenzied onslaught, first one step, then another. Several. A predatory grin split Marcsh's face as he bore down even harder, grunting and panting with tremendous effort, sensing that the end was near.

As soon as the Tone had sounded, Marcsh had withdrawn his sword and, instead of taking the Position, it had continued its blurred arc out and then down, aimed for the triangular juncture of Ronin's neck and shoulder. But almost simultaneously Ronin was lunging forward, shoulders twisting, and the blade whistled past him so close that he felt its hot wind. Thus extended, he slammed the heavy hilt of his still-sheathed sword into Marcsh's fists. He regained his ground and his blade flashed out.

The Bladesmen shifted in anticipation and excitement, crowding one another, craning their necks to see more clearly. They felt it in the air now, knew this was not an ordinary Combat.

Marcsh had stood, feet wide apart, knees slightly bent, sword before him. His knuckles were red and slick with blood and he glared at Ronin, hating him even more for the rebuke.

Ronin had faced him with his hip and his shoulder, right foot forward and extended, left behind him. He held his sword out at stomach level, point slightly higher than hilt.

Marcsh had leaped and again the blade flew down and Ronin caught it on the hilt, the heavy shock coursing through them both. They strained against each other, breath hissing through clenched teeth. The veins along Marcsh's thick biceps and inner forearms stood out, pulsing, from the muscles. His face and neck grew red with the effort.

He was extremely powerful, and he used his brute strength to break the deadlock, moving immediately into a series of horizontal thrusts, slashing and cutting. Ronin had parried it all, neither retreating nor advancing. Marcsh's close-set eyes blazed and his mouth opened with the heaving of his chest.

He had turned a horizontal slice into a feint, reversing his motion very rapidly but still having to overcome momentum, his weight working now against him, attempting to use his hilt as Ronin had before. The blade of Ronin's sword glinted and took the force of the attack, and he began a counter but Marcsh retreated. Sweat glistened along Marcsh's arms and down his sides and his shirt clung to him like a loose second skin.

And he had leaped forward, once more on the attack, and his sword lifted and fell, lifted and fell, his full power behind each stroke. The blade was a white blur obscuring the Combatants so that the Bladesmen were obliged to press closer in order to make out the course of Combat.

Still Ronin retreated under the assault, the shocks reverberating even into the first rows of onlookers, so that they imagined they could feel the terrific force being generated and were happy that they were merely watching. Motion blended as the attack resolved itself into the shape of repetition. The heavy blade lifted and fell, lifted and fell. Blue sparks flew upward and the constant clang of metal against metal was deafening. The air was acrid and leaden. Lifted and fell, lifted and fell, and time unraveled.

It was a form of hypnosis and not at all limited to Combat. That was its strength, because one tends to forget under the narrowed concentration of Combat. Narrower still is the deep concentration of the attack, of bringing Combat to its completion. And now Ronin saw it in Marcsh's eyes and he timed the counter perfectly, abruptly holding his ground as Marcsh, intent on the retreat as a gauge for his victory, swung again forward and down with all his strength. He came up on Ronin instantly, sword descending in a blur, eyes just beginning to open in surprise, as Ronin, feet planted firmly, bent into his knees, twisting his torso at the last possible instant. He pivoted his left foot away, and Marcsh, his body made ponderous and overbalanced by momentum, rushed past him. Ronin brought both arms around, following the pivot of his own momentum, using it, locking his elbows so that his arms were rigid with force, and smashed the flat of his sword against the daggam's back.

There came a cracking sound, muffled and thick, as

of the rending of a foundation under immense pressure, and Marcsh's body arched horribly, his arms thrust above his head in reflex, as if in supplication. His sword clattered to the floor. The body hit the floor with great force and was still. It lay there, unnatural and ugly, grotesque in its sudden parody of human form, as a great shout went up from the Bladesmen, and the Square of Combat was suddenly filled with milling people.

Ronin did not see the Instructor gesture but he heard over the tumult the clear Tone of the gong that signaled the end of Combat.

He stood and breathed deeply, the still center of a raging storm. He wiped sweat from his colorless eyes.

As if from far away he heard a voice cry, "Moment! Moment! I will have silence here!" The din continued. "Silence, I said!" roared the voice. The shouting died to low murmurings and then ceased altogether.

From his platform the Instructor glowered down at his students. "Stand silently where you are!" His face was red and his small eyes flashed. "This conduct is outrageous! Unthinkable! Rank Students would behave better. I shall not tolerate such an outburst in *my Class* again!" he bellowed at them. He pointed to two Bladesmen. "See to Marcsh." They bent to their task, trying to lift him gently, but a sound came from him so filled with agony that they left him and ran to fetch a litter.

Seeing this, the Instructor's gathering fury exploded, and he turned upon Ronin. "You fool!" he screamed, barely in control. "You have half killed him! How shall I explain that to his Instructor? How shall I explain that to his Saardin!" His voice had become shrill, rising in pitch. "This will reflect on me! On me! Do you understand what you have done! What gives you the idea you can use your weapon in such a manner?" He shook his fist at Ronin. He was trembling.

"As of this moment you are barred from this Combat Class, and I can assure you that it will be the same for all Classes, because I shall see to that personally. In addition, a full report of your irresponsible behavior shall be made to the Saardin of Security!"

There was a great tumult in the Hall now, sounds of voices and movement echoing and reechoing off the walls and ceiling, gaining in volume. Dimly, Ronin was aware of Nirren, somehow miraculously beside him in the crush.

The Instructor's voice rose to peak volume to be heard. "You will pay for this incident, and pay dearly!"

Ronin, adrenaline still pumping within him, crossed the line. He took a step forward and lifted his sword. "We will see who shall pay!" he yelled, but it was borne away on the tide of sound.

Nirren gripped him from behind. "Are you mad? What are you doing?"

Still Ronin advanced through the throng toward the elevated figure of the Instructor. Nirren clung to him, trying to gain a purchase to restrain him, as he fought his way through the tightly pressed, jostling bodies. They clung to Ronin like weights impeding his progress and he was only halfway there when he saw the Instructor, fearful now that he had quite lost control of the situation, wheel off the platform and, with his boy trailing in his wake, stride from the Hall.

Nirren got hold of him at last. The noise had increased and the heat was unbearable. He had to turn his head and stare at Nirren's working mouth before he understood, and even then it took a while. "Come on! Come on!"

Soon after, the Bladesmen came with the litter and bore Marcsh away.

"**T**HEY have all miscalculated."

"How do you know?"

He sighed. "I do not. It's a feeling."

"Based on something, surely. All the Saardin could not miss—"

He made a fist. "But they have, I know it! All they see are their own bits of power—"

"It is personal with them."

Nirren ceased his pacing long enough to stare at Ronin as he sat on the bed, stripping off his soaked shirt. "Why, yes, it could be put that way." He cocked his head quizzically. "You have been to see him then."

Ronin threw the shirt over a stool. "Yes."

Nirren stood in front of him, frowning. "But not to go back."

Ronin laughed humorlessly. "No, not at all."

"Were you not even tempted?"

Ronin looked up. "Well, he did try."

"Really."

"No need to worry about it."

Nirren relaxed somewhat. He looked at the bruise down Ronin's side. "I have sent for her," he said.

Ronin touched the bandage over the wound at his shoulder. There was still some pain. "That was hardly necessary."

He flicked a hand. "Nevertheless it has been done."

"Where is Stahlig?"

"Ah, attending to Marcsh, I believe," he said with a thin smile. "Why did you go then?"

"To see the Salamander?"

"Yes."

"Advice."

"From him?" Nirren laughed. "He is a Saardin. Why should he tell you the truth?"

"There are ties," Ronin said.

"Yes, and even after—"

"I expect so." Very quickly.

Nirren shook his head. "What did he tell you then?"

Ronin sat back on the pillows, resting. "That Borros is indeed mad."

"Did he? And how would he know that?"

Ronin took a pillow, wiped the sweat from his body. "He showed me a kind of proof." It left dark streaks on the fabric.

"What, exactly?" asked Nirren, his eyes watchful.

"What if I told you that Borros is not mad?"

"Are you?"

"I do not know."

"What of the Salamander's proof?"

"I talked to Borros myself."

"You will not tell me."

"I *am* telling you."

"Not about what he showed you."

Ronin threw the pillow from him. "How do you know he showed me anything?"

"Words would not have been sufficient."

Ronin nodded. "Yes." He went across the room and opened the wardrobe. "But I am not sure it *is* proof." He brought out a shirt with loose silk sleeves and no collar. "What do you think is Up there, above the Freehold?"

"What?" Nirren shrugged. "Nothing. Nothing worth talking about at least, unless you are partial to the idea of a kilometer of solid ice and snow. Why?"

He put on the shirt. "Because Borros believes that there is a civilization Up there, living in a land without ice or snow."

Nirren stared at him. "This is what he told you?"

"Yes."

"Did you ask him what he was working on?"

"It did not happen like that. I got what I could. But I am fairly certain of one thing. Freidal does not know much more than we do, otherwise Borros would not have been talking to anyone. Besides, at one point the Magic Man told me that he had not revealed anything of significance."

Nirren shook his head. "I can make sense of none of this. Surely nothing lives on the surface—the planet is too cold to sustain life."

"So it would seem."

"And where does that leave us?"

"It leaves *you* nowhere."

"Ah, Ronin—"

"I want no part of any Saardin."

"But you will try to see Borros again."

"Yes." He lifted a hand for a moment. "But because

I wish to do it." He sat on the pillows again. "What about your assignment?"

The Chondrin frowned. "It is a puzzle seemingly without a solution. Perhaps I am closer to my goal, perhaps not. Still, I cannot shake the feeling that—"

Ronin looked up. "What?"

"That there is more to it than any of us know." He ran his hand through his hair distractedly. "Sometimes —sometimes I could almost believe that there is a third force secretly at work—almost waiting for the other Saardins to make the first move."

"But there are only Saardins. Nothing beyond."

"Of course. That is what makes it so puzzling."

"And you have no facts."

Nirren sighed. "If I did, I would be with Estrille now."

"Have you told him?"

"Some."

"And?"

"He will not act without facts." He turned. "K'reen will be here at any moment."

"What of your Rodent?"

"What?" Nirren momentarily looked startled. "Oh —that is where I am off to now. Perhaps I am closer to finding him." He shrugged. "He is buried quite deep, that is the only fact of which I am certain at the moment. Do not be alarmed if you cannot locate me for a while—wait for me to contact you." And he was gone.

Ronin lay back on the pillows and waited for K'reen to come.

They came for him after Class, during first Spell, when there were less people about. He went with them without resistance because he was pragmatic enough to know that it had to come sooner or later, that they were just waiting for a valid excuse, because they hated him.

They marched swiftly through the Corridor and perhaps they were surprised that he came so willingly. Into a deserted Stairwell and Upshaft. To the Hall of Combat.

Empty shadows and dusty silence. Gray air hanging in sheets on the dim lights, bars of dark and light. The presence of ancestors unseen and forgotten, talking of bygone millennia, the descent into earth, a legacy of— what?"

"Draw it," grated the voice. "All my plans done in by you."

Korlik faced him while the others looked on. Perhaps Korlik wanted an audience. More likely they wanted to be here when it happened. He did not think about that.

"I wanted to go Upshaft with him more than anything else. Because of you—" It was as good as anything else.

Silence.

"Draw it," Korlik said again, grinding his teeth. "Come on." He waved his sword. "Well, what are you waiting for? Afraid?" He advanced. "All right, I'll show you what to do with this." He waved it again as he came on. "I am going to turn you around and shove this up you!"

Ronin unsheathed his sword and, for the next quarter Spell, turned aside all Korlik's attacks, standing his ground, refusing to counterattack.

Korlik bellowed in frustration and threw his sword

to the stone floor. Perhaps it was a signal, because they all fell upon him then and he went down. Someone tried to step on his neck and he grasped the ankle, twisted it violently until he heard the snap. They pummeled his stomach and tried to turn him over. He lifted his legs, straining against the tangle and the pressure, protecting his groin, and knew that he had to regain his feet now or they would have him pinned with his chest to the cold stone. They could not get a firm grip on his legs, and he did it, all the way up, gasping for air.

He found that Korlik and the others did not matter. He heard a low groan from somewhere near him. Korlik bent and retrieved his sword and, crouched, body shiny, advanced in an arc.

Ronin moved laterally but Korlik kept his sword point and body between Ronin and his weapon, shining dully on the stone, so that there were no more options—it had to be done. And the daydreaming was gone at once.

He rushed straight at Korlik, saw the wide blade raised, its size magnified, come whistling down, and knew that it would be all right because it was a vertical blow. He got in, past the point as it came arcing blurrily down, slammed his fist into the side of Korlik's head. And by the time Korlik had regained his balance and turned, he had the sword. He crossed a bar of light and it shone like silver.

But he was overconfident, buoyed by the success of the tactic, and he misjudged Korlik's recovery time and so was unprepared for the rush. He got his blade up but not enough, and the angle was all wrong, so that Korlik's sword cut through his like fabric. Korlik laughed when he saw the stumpy blade sheared through obliquely.

In truth he obviously did not get a good look at it in the dimness or he would certainly have been more cautious. As it was, he moved in, heedless of the shorn weapon still gripped tightly in Ronin's hand, and was thus surprised to feel it enter his chest.

Ronin had lunged, pushing the truncated blade in to the hilt, the force smashing Korlik against the wall, where he now stood, dark blood running all across him. Still he tried to get at Ronin, lurching up, pushing against the wall with his palm, then jerkily swinging his sword one last time, all coordination gone, before he toppled face down on the stone.

They left him there, standing over the corpse in the stillness, not daring to look into his dark and unreadable eyes.

And now he opened his eyes to find K'reen bent over him, face filled with worry. "I have heard about it," she said. "It is all over the Sector." She looked at him, pushing aside his shirt. "At least you were not hurt, and the wound has not reopened." She sat beside him. "What will happen now?"

He shrugged. "It is not so serious."

"But banished from Combat—?"

He sat up. "If what Nirren is concerned about happens, it will not matter."

"I do not—"

"The Saardins."

"Oh. Yes. What does he say? I so rarely see him now except at Sehna."

"The two factions appear to be very close to a confrontation—but this is nothing you do not already know."

"He is with Estrille then."

"No. He has been given a special assignment."

She went across the room to the mirror of beaten brass, hanging on the wall at head height, just over the cabinet. "It is near to Sehna," she said.

Ronin thought: Not enough time to see if Stahlig is through treating Marcsh.

She began to put up her hair, glancing at him from time to time in the mirror. "What is it that makes you so sad?" she said abruptly.

He sat on the edge of the pillows. "Why do you ask me such questions?"

"Because—" Her eyes stole away from his in the mirror and she touched a hand to her face. "Because I love you."

He caught the glint of the tears rolling slowly from the corners of her eyes. "What are you doing?"

She turned away and squeezed her eyes shut. "Nothing." Water trembled, glistening along her lashes.

He went across to her and spun her around so that her hair, still unbound on one side, floated in a dark arc, momentarily obscuring her cheek.

"Why are you crying?" he asked with some anger.

With her free hand she wiped under her eyes, and he saw within them a brief hint of—fear? He could not be sure.

"I hate that. Why are you crying?"

Anger flared and the thing within her eyes was gone. "You mean I am not allowed to cry?" He turned away from her. "What is it with you?" Her eyes were magnified by the water. "Does it upset you when I show any emotion? *You* cannot, is that it? Because I accept that. *I* do. Can you understand that? Why must you act like this? I cannot under— Don't you ever feel anything? How is it when we go to bed? Is it just—biological?" She turned back to the mirror, put her head in her arms, leaning on the cabinet.

He went into the other room and began to change his clothes. After a time, K'reen raised her head and stared into the mirror. She wet her fingers with her tongue, wiped away the tearstreaks. Then she finished putting up her hair.

They had to walk farther down the Corridor than was usual because the Stairwell closest to his quarters was newly blocked by a slide of rotting concrete and brittle crusty orange metal. The next one was clear and they began their descent to Sehna, Ronin holding before them the flaming torch. The stairs were cracked and pitted and appeared to be little used. Once or twice they had to jump stumps of stairs that had crumbled or had been sheared away by some force.

They did not talk and perhaps that is why they heard the sound. It was very soft and came from somewhere in front of them. Ronin stopped immediately and held K'reen still with his free hand. Slowly he extended the torch in front of them. The stairs stretched downward to the landing where they doubled back on themselves. They were deserted.

There was silence. Dust motes danced in the flickering heat of the torch, writhing as they were consumed by the fire to which they were drawn.

They moved slowly downward and it came again. A low moan, a half whimper of pain.

They were at the landing. Around the turning, the Stairwell stretched darkly away. She started to say something but he cut her off. He strained his ears, thinking now not about the sound below them but— He heard it again and he was sure. At first he thought that the soft scrabbling noise he had detected at the threshold of hearing was the movement of the small animals that lived in the walls, which everyone heard in the soft silences. But the sound had come again, closer, and he knew it for the patient pad of boots, how many he could not tell, on the stairs above them.

He grabbed K'reen's hand and they fled down into darkness.

Abruptly, the whimpering seemed nearer. Ronin thrust the torch before them and saw that the entire inner wall of the Stairwell had collapsed and, for many Levels, a dark pit yawned vertiginously.

They pressed themselves against the secure outside wall, and saw a figure below them. Disheveled and filthy, long hair falling lankly down its back, dressed in rags without color, it huddled pitifully in a corner away from the pit.

He stepped closer, could now discern a wan face covered with muck and sweat. Haunted, frightened eyes stared back at him, the shivering flame from his torch reflecting in the enormous pupils. The figure shrank from him.

He bent slowly, touched it gently. "Who are you?" And then, "We will not harm you."

He heard the bootsteps on the stairs, nearer, and he stood, turning toward them, ears straining again to gather more information. K'reen had crouched down, close to the figure, trying to talk to it. And he heard her choked gasp.

"Ronin!"

He turned back, lofted the torch, saw that the figure's right arm was a stump, torn and clotted with dried blood and newly forming skin, so it was not as recent as he had at first thought. Shadows danced madly around them, the central pillar of the flame.

Then. In the hollow of the creature's neck a glint of metal. Slowly, carefully, so as not to alarm it, Ronin reached for it: a crusted square on a grimy chain. He rubbed his thumb across the surface and brought it into the light.

" 'Korabb; Neer; Ninety-Nine,' " he read.

K'reen said, "This is a Neer? But how— If she was assigned to the ninety-ninth Level, what is she doing this far Upshaft?"

"And with an arm recently taken off." He thought of the Neer in Stahlig's quarters. "The largest and most complex Machines are on that Level—"

"It's the lowest Level, isn't it?"

"Yes, and only the best Neers work Down there—"

Boots echoed more urgently along the walls, stopped at the landing above them. Ronin thought he could hear the low murmuring of voices.

"Ronin, who—?"

He put his finger to his lips, turned to the Neer, whispered, "Korabb, can you understand me?" The figure looked from him to K'reen and back again. It nodded, and at that moment he became aware that the Neer was a female. A combination of the uncertain light, her position, and her filthiness had prevented him from seeing her clearly.

The Neer raised a thin finger, nailless, the end torn and black with blood.

"Ronin. Ronin, you have reached the end!" a cold voice called from above. "We have come for you!" There came to them the grate of metal on stone, a singular sound that they could not mistake, and K'reen gasped, realizing what Ronin had understood all along: they were on their way to Sehna, and he was weaponless.

He felt something touch his shoulder. The Neer's finger pressed against him urgently. She pointed at him and then K'reen, then down into the pitch of the stairs.

He shook his head and said, "We cannot leave you; you will surely die here if we do. Do you understand?" She shook her head and her mouth worked soundlessly. It struck him then that something was wrong. Apparently it had occurred to K'reen also, for she reached out and gently opened the Neer's mouth. Her eyes grew round and frightened and she jerked her head, trying to pull away, but K'reen held her firmly.

"Oh, Frost!" she whispered, and involuntarily swallowed. Ronin looked, saw a mouth with teeth and gums and palate and a dark bit of flesh that was trying to move. Where the base of the tongue should have been. And was not.

K'reen let go of the mouth and turned her pale face to Ronin's. "What could have happened? How could this—"

"Ronin. Ronin, we know the Med is with you!" There was a mocking tone to the voice. "K'reen? Yes, K'reen, that is her name." There was scraping again

from above as someone shifted. "Do not delude yourself into believing that you will die quickly and honorably. No Bladesman's death for you, my friend. We
shall cut the tendons in the backs of your legs so that
you will stay and watch us while we find out what the
woman is made of. Cut your eyelids and we will all
take turns holding your head so that you get the best
view. We would not want you to miss a moment while
we see how many of us she can take!" And the voice
laughed, high and piercing and unpleasant. "I mean at
a time!" The laughter echoed about them and K'reen
shivered.

There was a sudden scuffle of boots and the still air
eddied, sending a chill through them. Ronin flipped
the torch away from them, down into the pit of the
Stairwell. Shadows became visible above them, shuf-
fling and moving. Red light from the torch played far
below them but they were wrapped now in darkness.

Hulking shapes advanced down the stairs, the
shadows closing in. Ronin counted four and knew that
there was little hope. Orange light flashed briefly on
an upraised sword and Ronin readied himself for the
desperate charge up the stairs.

A thin shadow blurred past him, hurled itself like a
bolt, leaping obliquely up the stairs, crashing into the
now quickly descending figures. The Neer!

There were shrieks, and for a terrible instant, a
clawing mass of arms, legs, and torsos were limned in
the shuddering illumination of the dying torch, and it
seemed as if the bodies hung suspended in the air.
Then they all hurtled into the black well of the pit,
gaping and irresistible. He tried to catch a glimpse of a
face, any face. The Neer's face. But the mass had

dropped out of sight and they heard very loud the sickening wet smacks like giant sacks ripped open far Downshaft, reverberating up the ragged sides of the pit.

K'reen huddled against the outer wall, her body convulsed in long racking sobs.

Ronin turned away from the well.

She came into his arms then and clung to him, trembling. "I cannot," she cried through the tears. "I cannot—" He stroked her hair and hugged her to him, learning something important about himself.

And in that crumbling twilight world, at the edge of a grinning death, with loss and destruction nearly triumphant, they held each other for a very long time.

Two

INTO THE ABYSS

THE elliptical stone slab, squat and changeless, dominated the darkness. He stood just inside the threshold, waiting for his pupils to dilate. They were still out there, around the sweep of the Corridor: daggam.

And Nirren had not been at Sehna.

Afterward, K'reen had left him to finish her Cycle's work on the Med Level. "It will be best for me," she said.

There was no light anywhere, and it was very quiet, so that he would have to be extremely careful in his movements. The surgery looked all right. The back cubicle was deserted.

In the Corridor, G'fand had caught him up.

"Going Upshaft?"

He nodded. "Back to my quarters."

"Do you mind if I accompany you part of the way?"

He did not see how he could avoid it. He was thinking only of Borros. Time was suddenly very important. "Come along then."

135

They passed a Stairwell and Ronin thought he could hear the lentitudinous drip of viscous fluid. They took the next one, climbing in silence for a time. There was a fine dust in the air and every now and then they heard small sounds from inside the walls.

G'fand cleared his throat. "I just—wanted to say that—umm—no one wanted to bring up the subject of Class at board. In case you were wondering."

"I was thinking on other matters."

"Oh. Well. Everyone was a bit worried because—you know—of you perhaps being out of Class and—"

"I appreciate your concern."

"We are *all* concerned," G'fand said carefully.

Ronin glanced at him and smiled thinly. "Yes. You can tell them then not to worry."

"But Combat is your life! I would be inconsolable!"

"You talk about it as if it were a disgrace," said Ronin. "I acted honorably. It is others who have bent the Code."

"But it is what the Instructor says that matters," G'fand protested, misunderstanding him.

"Only to some people."

"Yes," he said bitterly, "the ones that matter."

Another shadow; he moved silently and swiftly across the room, touched the wall. The hidden door opened and he stepped through.

The small room was as it had been before: the narrow beds, the low lamps, Borros.

He was sitting up now, staring down at the backs of his hands. The yellow hairless head whipped around on its long neck. The gray eyes were dull and expressionless. He stared again at his hands.

Ronin sat beside him. "Borros—"

"Go," said the Magic Man in a tired voice. "Go and tell your Saardin that the answer is still no. It can only be no." The long fingers strayed to his forehead, touched the fading Dehn spots. "Tell him that there is nothing left worth having. He has tried it all and failed. All the shiny bits gone—I can no longer remember. So his attempt to affiliate me fails, too. I cannot help him, even if I wanted to." He made a gesture. "Now go and report on what the Magic Man has said; perhaps he will believe you, he does not believe me."

"Borros, you must listen to me carefully," Ronin whispered. "I am not a daggam; Freidal is not my Saardin. Frost, look at me! I was here last Cycle. You were very ill."

The gray eyes glanced at him, dull gold in their depths. He laughed grimly. "That is what they call it now?" The eyes blazed briefly. "You do not fool me. Deceit without end; I expect it from him. But your time is up. Let him send in the next one; but you can tell him when you leave. It will not work. He has failed."

This did not sound like the man he had tried to talk to just a Cycle ago; the man whose life he preserved. And now he was worried because Borros no longer sounded like a madman. Freidal would recognize this immediately; perhaps he already had. Ronin himself could see that if the Magic Man had held on this long he would, finally, tell Freidal all that he wanted to know before he went mad, if the Saardin wanted the knowledge badly enough. Freidal could do it, he knew that.

"What can I do to convince you?"

Borros heard the urgency in Ronin's voice and he smiled thinly, secretively. "All right. I direct it. I ask, you answer. Any hesitation—any hint whatsoever that you are fabricating your answers—and it is over."

"We have no time for this." Ronin glanced at the door to the Corridor.

Borros shrugged, his lips curling. "It is the only way."

Ronin made a gesture. "Get on with it then, if it will satisfy you."

The gray eyes were cold and watchful, perfectly clear. "I did not say that it would."

Ronin made an exasperated noise.

"What are you?" Borros said shortly.

"A Bladesman."

"Who is your Saardin?"

"I have none."

The eyes narrowed. "What?"

"I am unaffiliated."

His hands were like white flowers against the dark fabric of the blanket. "An interesting response." His head jerked once, involuntarily. "Which faction will you side with?"

"Freidal is my enemy."

"Huh! Is that so."

"He has already tried twice to have me killed."

"Do you expect me to believe that?"

There were limits. Ronin grabbed the front of his shirt, jerked him forward until their faces were very close. "I should have let you die last Cycle. It does not appear to have been worth the effort to save you."

"Let me go."

Ronin sat back and the Magic Man pulled at the

bottom of his shirt. "Tell me," Borros said, "what happened."

Ronin recounted the Combat with Marcsh and a wistful smile creased the Magic Man's countenance. "You broke his back?" he asked. "Are you sure?"

Ronin shrugged.

The Magic Man closed his eyes briefly. "Oh, if it were so." He looked at Ronin. "Go on."

Ronin told him how he and K'reen had been forced to take a rarely used Stairwell because of the rubble, which, he believed now, had been planned; how they had found the Neer. "Her tag was marked 'ninety-nine' but I have no idea what she was doing that far Upshaft. She was—mutilated. Perhaps the loss of the arm had been an accident, but not the tongue. She—"

Gold flecks danced in the gray eyes, and the head twitched again. He shivered.

"We could not leave her, and in the end—"

The yellow head whipped from side to side. "I think I—"

"—she took them with her—"

"It cannot be."

"—down into the pit."

"No, it cannot— Her tag, you saw her tag. What was her name?"

"I do not see what—"

"Just do it!" Cold gray boring into him.

"Korabb," said Ronin. "Her name was Korabb."

And abruptly, like a sword being sheathed, the eyes softened. Then the head turned away. "Chill take them! What have they done?"

Ronin shook his head. "I do not understand any of this."

"Yes," the Magic Man said in a whisper. "I believe that."

"I believe at first they felt that I would never actually get so far as to actually be able to build it," said Borros quietly. "After all, Mastaad was there reporting on every step I took. In the beginning I paid him no notice, let him do as little as possible because that is the way I am. But he lacked patience and because of his single-mindedness I became suspicious.

"There are always stories, you know, of Security keeping track of all the Magic Men, but"—he lifted his hands—"one is never sure what to believe. But once I was sure that the construction was possible I became suspicious of everyone. Then I caught him going through my notes and I was sure. I threw him out and burned the notes.

"He could not read them, of course, but he already knew enough to tell them that I would build it. So they came in directly."

"But you said that this—Machine you had devised would be able to detect temperature and winds on the surface. Why—?"

"Why are they so afraid? Because it would have proved that there is life Up there. Human life. They do not want that."

He sighed. "The old order is entrenched in its power. Never mind the confrontation. If it happens it will not matter who is victorious. The Saardins are secure in their control over all the peoples of the Freehold. The ancient patterns have been set; they are changeless. If war comes, there will be destruction and loss of life. But then there will be stabilization, and the structure will remain."

He stared at Ronin. "Imagine what would happen if people knew that there were men on the surface, that it could support life. There would be a movement to go Up, open the Freehold, live Above. That would blow everything apart, and their power would be gone. Confined here, we have no choice."

"But we are slowly dying," Ronin said. "That surely must be obvious to them."

Borros nodded. "Oh, it is. But it is a death by slow attrition. As they view it, death may not truly come for a century, perhaps two. By then—" He shrugged. "They live in an eternal present." The hands moved over the dark blanket.

"I have seen the surface," said Ronin.

"Ah."

"A Machine called a Lens. The surface is—covered in ice and snow. Completely."

The Magic Man smiled without warmth. "Above us, yes. The ice is quite solid for a kilometer or more I believe, although there is no real way of determining that. But I have learned that the Freehold is located near one end of the planet"—he gestured—"like this, and we are here, near the top. Ice covers the planet at top and bottom. Millennia ago it was more confined, I believe, now it covers more of the planet. But not all. You see? Near the center it is warmer, the land is brown, the sun shines out of a clear sky and heats the land and the people."

"How do you know this?"

Borros shrugged again. "It is all pointless, this knowledge, for before long we will all of us—Freehold and surface dweller alike—be destroyed."

"You spoke of this when you—"

"Yes, you were here, saw the state I was in. I was then more susceptible to the emanations."

"It was—I felt a kind of presence."

The Magic Man nodded. "Entirely possible. There have been Cycles lately when it was certainly strong enough."

"But what is it?"

"As yet I cannot answer that. I have not the knowledge."

"It is real."

"Oh, yes. Just, I believe, a long way off."

"And now—?"

"Now we both have a decision to make. I must get to the surface, to the people Above. There is very little chance that this—force can be stopped. But I must try. And so, I believe, must you." He said it rather smugly. Ronin disliked him, did not trust him, and yet he knew that he was right. It was irksome.

The thin, frosty smile came again, unpleasant and inevitable. "I see that I am correct. All right. It is settled. Now for the second part. Before we attempt to leave, you must go Downshaft."

The smile dissolved like ice in a hearth. "You must go," he said slowly, "below the ninety-ninth Level."

"I have no ink," he said, pricking it. "I will give you the best description I can but I am afraid that my knowledge is limited." The blood oozed out as he squeezed the finger. "Still, it is better than nothing." And he began to draw on the fabric.

Ronin had said, "But the ninety-ninth is the lowest

Level. Below that is the rock foundation of the Free-hold."

"Another deception," Borros said didactically. "They are quite expert at it. The remnants of another civilization—the civilization of our ancestors—lies below the Freehold. I am quite sure. I know because Korabb went there.

"She was my wife. They told me she was dead, killed while working on one of the massive Energy Converters. Shredded beyond a hope, they said. That was six Sign ago, and all that time I believed—" He shook his head. "I do not know what I believed."

"But what happened?"

"I shall never know. But my opinion is— Look, ten Cycles before they reported her death, she told me that she had found what she believed to be an entrance to a world below the Freehold on the ninety-ninth Level.

"I was beside myself with excitement. Why, when I thought of the secrets, the knowledge that such a world might contain! They couldn't very well have burned everything—some books and plans that had been brought Up, yes, but not the actual Machines themselves.

"I knew I could never get to that Level myself, so I urged her to do a bit of exploring on her own. She made one brief foray Down there and I knew I had been right.

"I believe now that they must have caught her going Down there a second time. They would have wanted to know what she found. Freidal would want that very much; you saw how much. Perhaps they let her go, afterward."

There was a silence for a while. Ronin watched the Magic Man's movements on the scrap of fabric.

"The answer to what comes is Down there," Borros said. "I know it. You must find it and bring it back. Only then can we leave." He continued to draw. "It is written on a scroll; written in peculiar glyphs. Here, I am writing glyphs in that mode so that you will recognize them. The scroll will have a heading. Look, this is it. That is all I know. It will tell us much about that which comes, perhaps even describe a method of defense. Who knows?" He shrugged again, and looked up for the last time. "It is our only hope." And gave him the scrap of fabric, stiff now with the drying blood.

"And, Ronin," he said blandly, "try to get back before they rend me to pieces."

THE panel seemed easy enough to understand; if only it worked.

They heard the sounds of boots, soft voices, indistinct but drawing closer from beyond the Corridor's turning.

Ronin pressed a button and the Lift's massive metal doors slid shut, sealing them in a velvet blackness and total silence.

"We are not moving."

He groped in the darkness, pushed a sphere marked for ninety-five. Close enough. It glowed a cold blue and they began to descend.

He had been in one before and immediately he knew it was all wrong. Instead of the steady humming descent, the Lift plunged in jerks and starts, so that they had trouble keeping their footing and were forced to brace themselves against the walls.

They continued to drop with increasing speed now and the vibrations became more pronounced, the swinging of the Lift more erratic.

145

They felt the lurch then and their stomachs seemed to rise sickeningly. They felt light. The cable had snapped, he realized. They were hurtling down the Lift shaft at tremendous speed. Their ears blocked, and he heard a moaning beside him.

There was a time when he would not have been able to tell. Certain fundamentals had to be pointed out, explained, and then incorporated so that they became reflexive. And then it was a matter of sharpening the instincts. It took time.

He stood at the threshold of his quarters and knew someone was inside. He realized it as he was reaching for the Overhead panel. He left the rooms dark and, conscious that he was a perfect silhouette in the glow of the Corridor Overheads, went swiftly, silently in.

Across the room, hanging on the wall, was his scabbarded sword. It seemed very far away.

He went across to it and no one stopped him. Slowly he withdrew the blade, keeping the doorway to the rear room in his line of vision.

He came into the rear room very quickly, crossing the threshold and lighting the Overheads simultaneously, his sword above his eyes to shield them from the first bloom of the light.

G'fand blinked at him, squinting. He wore dark leggings and a light shirt of heavy material.

"What are you doing here?" Ronin said with some annoyance, to cover his relief.

The Scholar was pale and drawn, as if he had not slept for some time.

"I came to talk to you. To tell you something." Despite his obvious tiredness, there seemed a certain resolution about him, perhaps in the way he stood, which Ronin had not seen before.

"Why are you hiding back here then?"

"I heard someone about to come in and I suddenly thought that it might be K'reen."

Ronin could not help smiling. "I am quite sure she would have understood."

G'fand flushed slightly. "I—it might have been embarrassing."

Ronin turned and went into the larger room. G'fand followed.

Ronin lit the Overheads and took the scabbard off the wall, strapped it on. "Tell me what is so important."

G'fand ran his fingers through his long hair. "I cannot bear to be here a moment longer. I must leave. I know what you must think! But at least you can understand why I must go. If leaving means freezing on the surface, then I tell you I find that preferable to the living death of the Freehold. At least I shall be free for a time, my own master. Here, I am encased, unable to breathe."

Unaccountably, Ronin found himself thinking of the Salamander's vast library. Rows and rows of books that G'fand would never have an opportunity to read.

"Calm yourself," he said. "I do not think you truly mean that."

"But I do!" There was a sadness now in the Scholar's voice. "You are like all the rest. You do not think I am a man. But I have some proficiency with weapons now—I can use sword and dagger—"

"And how will you eat?" Ronin asked, reaching

into the high wardrobe and withdrawing a light mailed corselet.

"With these," G'fand said proudly. From under his shirt he produced two bands wide enough to fit snugly around a man's upper arm.

Ronin paused. "Food bands. Where did you get those?"

"I stole them. And do not worry, they will not be missed."

Ronin donned the metal corselet. "You are serious then?"

G'fand nodded. "That I am."

Abruptly something the Scholar had said floated up from the recesses of his mind: *I have partially deciphered the glyphs of the very ancient writing.* It had meant nothing to him at the time, but now—

"A journey is what you need. Is that correct?"

G'fand gave him a puzzled look. "Ronin, I must get out now—this Spell."

He took something out of the wardrobe, held it in his hand. "Come with me instead."

"With you? But what—?" The Scholar was staring at the food band Ronin was holding. He watched, fascinated, as Ronin worked it onto his arm.

"What do you say? I leave now."

"But where—? I don't—"

"With luck, out of the Freehold. I will explain it on the way. Fetch your weapons." He reached for his dagger.

The close air was filled with a high keening sound that wavered in tone but built in intensity. The Lift shook as it dropped, trying to shake itself apart.

Ronin pressed the other floor spheres on the panel in front of him. They lit up in twos and threes as his fingers touched them. The Lift continued its mad flight, their cold blue glow mocking.

He remembered, then. The red sphere at the top of the panel. He hit it.

The Lift slammed to a halt and their legs buckled like fabric. The car hung, quivering, suspended in the shaft, the broken cable above them singing as it snaked onto the top of the Lift. Ronin regained his feet, took several deep breaths. G'fand was still on his haunches, sobbing in great lungfuls of air.

"Ronin, we—"

"No time. We have got to get out of here quickly. I have no idea how long this brake will hold." His hands worked at the panel but the doors remained shut. He drove his fingers at the center seam of the doors. "Come on! We must open it up."

G'fand was on his knees. He put his hands on his thighs and lifted his head. Sweat had matted his long hair across his forehead and along his cheeks. He looked as if he were bound to the floor.

"We—we almost died—"

"G'fand, the doors!"

"Crushed like vermin—bones to jelly—" His eyes were glazed; he was dazed by the force of his imagination.

Ronin turned and pulled him to his feet, attempting to transmit some of his strength. "G'fand, we are not dead!" Their faces were very close. "But we soon may be unless we get out of here! I cannot do this myself. I need your help."

His eyes focused then. "Yes. Yes. We will open the doors. The two of us."

They dug their fingers into the center seam, both pulling from the same side. They heaved and strained until their arms ached and their stretched shoulder joints burned and the water rolled down their faces and into their eyes, making them sting and clouding their vision. Muscles popped and their legs stiffened with the effort. They clenched their teeth and the cords along their necks stood out.

And minutely they felt the door move. They panted like animals but speech was too much added effort and they pulled with renewed determination. And slowly, slowly, the door slid back.

They stooped when it was open wide enough for them to get through, dropped their arms, which felt as heavy as iron, and gasped at the air. Their mouths were dry.

They looked up then and found that they were between Levels. But they were in luck. Perhaps a meter above them beckoned the open entrance to a Level, the protective doors having been sheared away at some previous time, stumps hanging like rotted teeth.

There came an ominous groaning as of tortured metal, and the Lift lurched sickeningly. Ronin put his hands together and G'fand stepped onto them, launching himself upward until he could grasp the lip of the entrance. The groaning came again and he strained, lifting one knee, finally levering himself up onto the Level.

The Lift lurched again and, below him, Ronin's ears were filled with a metallic shrieking. The Lift trembled and slid and he saw the walls of the shaft rise as the brake began to give way. The Lift lurched sideways, caught on a protrusion in the shaft, and Ronin coiled his body and leaped. The screaming of hot metal was all that he could hear. His fingers caught the lip of the Level, but one hand, slick with sweat, slid off and he hung for a moment, swinging with unwanted momentum by one arm until G'fand reached down, grasped the free hand, and pulled up. He felt the Lift shudder once again and the top of the car slid down. He pushed with his arms, propelling himself onto the Level, and G'fand pulled him from the lip of the entrance, as with a terrible grinding the Lift plummeted down the shaft, the car's top several centimeters from cutting Ronin in two.

They were assaulted by the combined stench of rotting garbage, excrement, and myriad unwashed bodies. The odor grew as they passed doorways, black and gaping. G'fand peered into one and gasped, choked. Ronin held his breath and pulled him quickly back. Still he caught a glimpse of white bone, a staring human eye, blackness where the other should have been. There was the impression of much movement along the floor, the sounds of soft scuttling.

"Where are we?" G'fand whispered.

Ronin shrugged. "Far Downshaft, anyway."

"What do we do now?"

"Find another way Downshaft to the ninety-ninth." He pointed. "We will try this way."

The Corridor curved away from them, dim and grimy with disrepair. Ronin thought, Could we be as far Down as the Workers' Levels? The Overheads were going. They glowed dismally, sputtering at spots, completely burned out at others. Apparently they had been dark for some time, because torches crackled and flared in makeshift niches carved crudely into the walls. So what light there was was a bizarre blend of fiery orange and cold blue-white.

They paused once to listen but all they could hear was the background drone of dripping water and tiny scurrying feet.

They went quickly and quietly. The walls here had lost all semblance of color. Theoretically all Levels were color coded so that one could tell at a glance what Level one was on. But these walls were covered with a thick coating of filth onto which obscene words and grotesque pictures had been drawn or roughly carved. Their obvious anguish was appalling.

They spied no one. Now and again they passed cracks in the ceiling and walls, extended networks of neglect, the damage once or twice so extensive that the sections on either side no longer matched. Several times they were obliged to clamber over blocks of rubble where parts of the Corridor had collapsed. The light grew perceptibly dimmer.

Ronin paused, extending an arm, holding G'fand back. He peered ahead. They went forward slowly about six meters and stopped abruptly.

It looked as if a gigantic fist had smashed into the Corridor. Something apparently had exploded with tremendous force from the inner Well, tearing open the wall, crumbling the floor for a space of a meter and a half. They peered cautiously into the gaping hole. There appeared to be a fire burning below on what they took to be the next Level.

G'fand wiped at his forehead. "Frost!" he whispered. "What is happening?"

Ronin said nothing. He looked across the face of the pit.

"Perhaps we should see if we can help."

"These Levels appear to be deserted," Ronin said somewhat distractedly.

"Still—"

"Our problem is how to cross this pit. There is nothing we could do in any event."

G'fand looked up out of the flickering light. "Why not retrace our steps and traverse the Corridor from the opposite direction?"

"Too much time lost, and the Corridor might be in worse repair. We press onward here; there is no turning back."

He stepped into the dark of the blown wall and, after a moment, called to G'fand. He had found a metal beam, set free of its foundations by the collapse. They set to work maneuvering it through the gap in the wall and setting it down in the Corridor. Then they pushed it across the diameter of the pit, found that it was long enough to reach the floor on the other side. He stood on it, bounced slightly, testing it.

He went first. It was narrow, barely seven centimeters wide, but it was twisted very little, so that the surface was fairly smooth and even.

The pit blossomed before him, lurid orange light twisting in the darkness like a bloated serpent, alive and deadly far, far below, swinging in short arcs, light receding and approaching, forming patterns. And vertigo lapped at the edges of his vision, waves forming. After that he did not look into the depths, but concentrated on his booted feet as they inched along the beam. One step at a time. Centimeter by centimeter, arms outstretched for balance. And at last he was across.

He turned and beckoned to G'fand, who stepped up on the beam and moved out over the pit.

Ronin called to him: "Concentrate on your movement; feel your feet against the metal. That's right, one at a time. Slowly now. Careful, feel your balance. There. Now."

G'fand was almost halfway across when his back foot slipped as he put his weight on it and he lurched to one side, over the yawning pit. He fell. And reached up desperately, in reflex, one hand hitting the beam, the fingers finding purchase. He swung dizzyingly in short arcs, his other hand scrabbling to find the beam.

Ronin first thought of pushing himself out on his stomach to get to him, but he did not trust the beam to hold them both and there was no time to find out. "G'fand," he called, "let your legs hang, do not move them, you must stop the swing. All right, now reach up. No, to the left. Yes, more; now stretch."

G'fand now gripped the beam with both hands, and hung like a vertical bar, arms stretched above him. He looked at Ronin. Hair was in his eyes and he shook his head in an attempt to free his vision, and his slippery hands skidded on the metal. He caught himself just in time.

"Easy, easy," said Ronin. "Listen to me, G'fand, and do exactly as I tell you. Put one hand in front of the other. Look up, not down." The strain showed on the Scholar's face. "Good. Now again. Think of only the next movement. One at a time. Good. Again." He spoke to him in a steady stream and in this way G'fand made his painful way across the remaining length of the beam, until, reaching out, Ronin was at last able to pull him up from the edge of the abyss. G'fand's body shook and he turned away from Ronin and was violently sick.

And now dark smoke and choking fumes rose in thin swirling clouds from the Level below. And now the fitful glow appeared brighter through the gaping rent. And now they heard the muffled pounding of running feet, and under it a dry, crackling sound, abnormally distinct and clear on the close air.

Ronin, crouched along one slimy wall, dragged G'fand along the Corridor, well clear of the rubble surrounding the hole. He pulled him off the floor and said, gently, very close to his face, breathing the sour smell, "I am sorry but we must move on—at once."

G'fand wiped his mouth and nodded. "Yes, yes," he whispered. "I am all right."

They moved on as swiftly as they could.

Presently they encountered the first people either of them had seen on this Level. They were all dead. Bodies were strewn about the Corridor as if hurled through the air by some titanic force. They lay burned —some so badly that they could not make out their features—maimed and broken, amid viscous puddles of dark seeping blood.

G'fand stared wide-eyed. "By the Chill! What has happened here?"

Ronin said nothing, and they plunged on into the murk of the curving Corridor, away and away, over the stinking mounds of the bodies. No Bladesmen here, and Ronin knew that he had been right; they were far Downshaft, among the Workers.

He paused as a small indistinct shape fled from out of a doorway, running at full speed into him. He grabbed hold, almost losing his balance, and looked down to see a small girl struggling in his arms. He picked her up and looked closely at her, the first sign of life they had encountered on this Level. She had thin pinched features visible intermittently beneath long lank hair whippping about as she writhed against his grip. She was sobbing, and through her tears Ronin saw that her eyes held a measure of torment that startled him.

"Are you hurt?" he asked, but she would not or could not answer.

G'fand touched Ronin and pointed ahead. A figure had reeled out of the doorway from which the girl had run. A tall gaunt woman with short hair and a hungry mouth and dull eyes. She saw them.

She ran unsteadily toward them. She screamed, "What are you doing to her?" She rushed down the Corridor at them. The child cringed and screamed as the woman reached out one long clawlike hand, dirty, the nails broken far down their length. The child clung to Ronin with a strange desperation. Then the woman took her.

She raised her right hand, brandishing a long curved blade, crusty with dried blood. "Animals! You're not content with me, you take her too—"

"She ran into—" Ronin began, but the woman was not listening.

"Taking her off to some dark room, were you? Get away!" she screamed, and whirled, pulling the girl behind her back along the Corridor, disappearing through the doorway from which they both had emerged. Ronin still felt the clutch of the girl, felt from far away his lost sister's arms around him.

He began to run, calling, "Come on!" over his shoulder, and heard G'fand coming after him. Bursting through the doorway.

Dim and smoky. Rooms much smaller than Upshaft. Three rooms to a quarters, two or three families. The rooms were a shambles. Broken furniture, shards of pottery, ripped fabric, the floor slippery-sticky with an indistinguishable amalgam of liquids. Nothing moved here and they went on into the second.

Ronin saw an arm protruding from a pile of refuse. He drew his blade and uncovered the body. It was a Worker, thick chest and arms, squat. By his outstretched hand was a heavy lever, ripped from a Machine, obviously used as a club. He turned the body. The Worker's chest was a pulpy mass and there was so much blood that they could not count the number of times he had been stabbed.

"Frost!" he muttered. "Have they all gone mad?"

G'fand turned his head away.

They moved into the last room. A lamp burned, hung from the ceiling, swaying slightly so that shadows moved and perspective was shattered.

The woman knelt on a bed at the rear wall. A washstand had been knocked over. The woman grasped the sobbing girl in one hand, and with the other arm, the hand still gripping the blade so hard that the knuckles were white, she held a limp figure to her. Her eyes were wide and staring blankly. A thin line of spittle drooled from a corner of her mouth. They paused just inside the doorway.

"Fiends!" she cried. "One more step an' you'll get what your friend out there got!"

G'fand stared at her and choked. "You did that?"

She laughed, a throaty, chilling sound, and her eyes rolled madly in their sockets. The girl struggled to get free. "Aye, that. Surprised, are ya, well so was he!" Her eyes wavered and dropped for an instant to the head of the small figure she was cradling.

"See," she wailed. "Look upon your work! Fiends' work!" And she turned the limp figure, and they saw a thin young boy, perhaps somewhat older than the girl, same dark pinched features. "See how you have defiled my son! See how you have taken his life!" Her voice rose, and quickly she clutched the boy back to her. Strength seemed to flood into her then, and she drew herself up defiantly. "You'll get no satisfaction here! Not this time!"

Too late Ronin realized that she had spied his drawn sword. Too late he divined her intent. She pulled the girl to her, the child's eyes round and staring, a high keening coming from her open mouth, and as Ronin leaped she drew the long curving blade across the girl's trembling throat. A gout of blood erupted and the keening became a thick gurgle, and she twisted the body behind her so that he fell atop her.

But the blade was now behind him, out of his line of vision. He dropped his sword to free his hands. He twisted to find the knife before it found him.

He was aware of her arm moving swiftly and then he felt her convulse violently under him, arched and stiffened. A smile came to her face at the same time the trickle of blood did. He looked down to see the knife plunged hilt deep into her side. He tried to withdraw it, but her fist, locked in a death grip, would not give up the hilt. A kind of relief suffused her face. Then he felt a spreading wetness, hot and sickening.

He backed off the bed on his knees. A sudden dizzyness threatened to overwhelm him. Reflexively, he retrieved his sword. G'fand moved to the edge of the bed. "What—?" But Ronin waved him wordlessly away. "Out!" he managed to gasp.

"But—"

"Out!" he bellowed. And they stumbled through the reeking rooms out into the Corridor, raced along its curving length.

They almost overran the familiar bulge of a Lift's doors, and heaving them apart they pitched inside, closing the doors behind them.

In warm darkness they sat, panting, and listened to the soft silence as their pulses slowed and breathing returned to normal. It seemed like a long time.

Presently Ronin heard G'fand stir.

"I have that trapped feeling again, as if the walls are closing in on me. The Freehold is dying, it's all coming apart." He shifted. "How far Downshaft are we?"

Ronin stood and moved his fingers over the Lift's control panel. He pressed a sphere and the doors opened, closed again. "According to the Lift, the seventy-first Level. Perhaps we can take it all the way to the ninety-fifth."

"Is that all you can think of," G'fand said accusingly, "after all we have witnessed. The Lower Levels are going—the Workers murdering one another—total madness!"

There was no response from Ronin. "By the Chill, you are like ice," G'fand said bitterly. "Nothing affects you! We have just seen things that have wrenched my stomach. What flows through your veins? Surely not blood!"

Ronin looked down at him, his colorless eyes barely discernible, and said, "You are free, as you always were, to return Upshaft, to attempt even to reach the surface."

G'fand put his head down and would not meet Ronin's gaze. Their harsh breathing was all that could be heard for a while.

When he was certain that G'fand would stay, he punched the sphere marked "ninety-five." It glowed and they commenced to sink rapidly and smoothly Downshaft. G'fand stood up. The Lift hummed. Ronin drew his dagger. The Lift sighed to a halt. The doors opened soundlessly.

He had assumed that since no Lift they had been in went as far as the ninety-ninth Level, they would be obliged to take a Stairwell the rest of the way. He saw now that he had been mistaken.

There was no Corridor. They stood instead upon a metal-grillwork scaffold arcing away from them on either side until it was lost to view in the haze.

Space. Where the inner wall of the Corridor should have been was enormous space. Ronin had never seen so much open space. G'fand stared with his mouth partly open.

They moved slowly to the low metal railing that ran

around the inner edge of the scaffolding. And looked down.

Immense geometric shapes, some simple, others extremely complex, all stupefying in size, studded the vast gallery below them. And now Ronin knew why the Lifts descended only as far as the ninety-fifth Level. They were peering down into an area four Levels high. Perhaps the sides of the gallery themselves were Machines. The life of the Freehold, he thought. Without these we die.

A deep humming filled the air, permeating it so that it seemed to flutter before their eyes. Soft blue haze hung in the air, trembling minutely. Light came from an unidentifiable source, lost somewhere above them. It was very warm, and a sharp, pungent smell, not at all disagreeable, floated on the air. Over the droning of the Machines they could just make out, now and then, the faint chatter of voices. Oddly, the sound heartened them.

They began to walk along the scaffold and at length they came upon a square opening cut into the outer edge abutting the sheer wall. Ronin looked down. A vertical ladder stretched away into the haze. It appeared clear. They descended, Ronin holding the dagger in his mouth, teeth locked on the hilt. As they went, they passed other scaffolds at regular intervals. They were deserted. He counted seven before they reached the floor of the gallery.

The thrumming was more insistent here, seeping up through the soles of their boots into their legs. The close air smelled of artificial heat and what Ronin knew to be lubricant. He had smelled it enough on Neers. The Machines rose all about them, a lush humid forest, strange and compelling. The light was dimmer, the blue haze thicker.

Off to their left, three Neers stood debating, their voices smeared by the background sounds._ The air hung like sheets.

They hunkered down by the purring side of a Machine, aware of its warmth, and Ronin unfolded the crude map the Magic Man had drawn for him. G'fand ate several mouthfuls of food while Ronin studied the piece of fabric.

The trouble was that the map had been drawn assuming that they had come to the ninety-ninth Level via the designated Lift, the one that had failed. Although he knew in which direction they had gone on the seventy-first Level, he had only a rough idea of the distance they had traveled before coming upon the second Lift. The map covered very little of the geography of the ninety-ninth Level. He would have to estimate the difference in their position, a dangerous but necessary action.

G'fand, still chewing, wiped a greasy hand across his mouth and rubbed it on his breeches. He swallowed. "Do you know where we have to go?"

Ronin pointed away from the group of gesticulating Neers. "This way. No noise."

They slipped from Machine to Machine, the bulky shapes looming out of the haze to offer transitory shelter. He took them on a zigzag course out across the floor of the gallery.

Rapidly the walls receded from their view, and G'fand, glancing up, fancied they were adrift in an ephemeral, forbidding world. He felt an odd discomfort without the security of walls about him.

They had covered almost a kilometer and had begun to sweat profusely in the damp heat, when Ronin brought them to a halt. In the shadow of a squat Machine they stood very still and listened to the voices just ahead of them.

"This is leading nowhere."

"Don't I know it! We've been here for over a Spell. Are you certain you checked the generator in Block Twelve?"

"Checked and rechecked. If there is any connection it is beyond me."

"Beyond all of us, I am afraid."

There came the sounds of metal against metal, a light scraping, and then a sigh.

"I don't know. What if we tried the second Level with *all* the power on?"

"Um, it might work at that. Just make sure—"

The conversation receded as they crept away. Following their short detour around the Neers, they resumed their oblique course across the gallery.

The huge circular Machine stood at the end of a broad area, wider than most of the spaces between the hulking shapes. They dared not approach it directly for fear of being detected either by Neers or by daggam.

They moved cautiously along a narrow aisle parallel to the one leading to the Machine. The heat increased and they had to will themselves not to pant. They were obliged to stop twice to let Security patrols pass them on perpendicular but intersecting routes. Each time Ronin waited long minutes after they had passed before proceeding. Once they almost ran into the back of a daggam who stepped out into their aisle, and they shrank back into the shadows, waiting breathlessly until he moved away.

Crouching low, they made their way, skirting the Machine, until, having seen it from all sides, Ronin judged the way to be clear. Once more he consulted the map, to be certain that they approached it from the right direction. They moved toward it.

It cast its own long shadow, the promise of a haven, a towering structure of incomprehensible function, wider at the bottom than the top, all sharp angles and crenelations. Light flashed along its summit, smoky in the haze. It seemed to be vibrationless.

They paused in the meager shadow of a small Machine about to make the final approach. Ronin held them there. It did not feel right. They sweated.

Three daggam converged on the Machine that was their goal. Their conversation dissipated on the active air. Presently, they split up, went out of his sight. Still he waited.

A black cloud bloomed to their left, the way they had come. A crash filled the air and they felt the floor tremble slightly beneath them. They heard the sound of running feet. They ventured a look. The cloud had ballooned out, staining the haze. Lemon flame licked below it.

"What happened?" G'fand whispered.

Ronin smiled thinly. "I believe the two Neers we passed knew less about that Machine than they thought." He saw daggam running toward the fire, and touched G'fand.

They dashed across the open area and into the shadow of the towering Machine marked on the Magic Man's map. Ronin put a palm flat against the metal side. It was still. Perhaps it was the structure's quiescence that had led Korabb to begin her clandestine exploration. They moved along the side.

It did not look like an entrance but then it did not look like much of anything save a wall of metal. There was a wheel to turn, it was that simple. Ronin turned it withershins as far as it would go. A disc approximately a meter and a half wide was now raised from the surface of the Machine. They grasped the right edge of the ellipse and pulled. An opening yawned before them.

Without hesitation Ronin stepped in; G'fand followed. As soon as they were across the threshold, the oval closed of its own accord.

They were in impenetrable blackness.

A vertiginous sense of space, echoing minutely. Silence, almost. A damp rich smell. Far away, a sound: persistent but so very distant that it was indefinable: a kind of seething.

G'fand fumbled out his tinder box and lit a torch he produced from his belt.

An oval tunnel danced before them, black with age. Underfoot the floor sloped gently downward. They went down into the dark and presently they began to feel a chill breeze on their faces and G'fand was obliged to protect the now-whipping flame from extinguishing. Beads of moisture clung to the walls and fairly soon they encountered cones of what appeared to be ice growing down out of the ceiling. Some were mottled gray but others contained streaks of orange and light green, magenta and deep blue. They became more numerous until Ronin and G'fand had the discomforting sensation of being turned upside down, as if they were walking on the ceiling instead of on the floor.

At first they had paused every so often to listen behind them until Ronin was satisfied that they had not been observed entering the portal and that there was no pursuit. After more than half a Spell, the tunnel commenced to slant more sharply downward and they had to be more careful of their footing. The walls grew slimy and different in texture and Ronin had G'fand bring the light closer to the side. Masses of a gray-blue lichen completely covered the walls, glinting oddly in the light.

Ronin told G'fand to gut the flame. At once they were engulfed in an eerie bluish glow. "The lichen is phosphorescent," G'fand exclaimed. "I have seen the like in some of the food-growing vats. It's thrown away." They found that they had to get used to the new light. Light colors—G'fand's shirt for instance, where the fabric showed through the grime and dried sweat—jumped out disconcertingly; other dark colors vanished altogether unless one was very close to them.

The low seething sound that had been with them since they first entered the tunnel grew more distinct although they were still at a loss to define it.

They paused once to eat and rest, pulling at the tough pressed food from the bands, backs against the cushiony walls, legs stretched out before them. They talked of inconsequential matters, deliberately avoiding certain topics that were all too much on their minds.

They resumed the march and presently the sound increased in volume with such a rush that they felt as if they had opened an unseen door. It washed over them, reverberating down the tunnel, and they perceived a slight change in the light.

Just ahead they found a gigantic aperture in the wall to their right. There was a glow beyond; colored lights swam. A promontory beckoned to them.

They looked out into a cavern so vast that it seemed to have no end. Streaks of pastel light drew themselves upon the air, and by their uncertain illumination Ronin and G'fand were able to make out the enormous arch of the waterfall thundering out from a rock face, cascading down in a froth of turbid silvery spray into the bed of a snaking river glinting far far below. The echoing boom of the kinetic water reflected back at them like a physical presence enfolding them. They stood transfixed at the sight.

G'fand said something but Ronin could not hear him for the noise. He leaned closer and repeated, "I never knew such a thing still existed. I had read—it is something out of legend!"

Ronin turned to him. "Time to go," he yelled over the roar.

Apparently the glowing lichen needed a great deal of moisture in order to survive, for as they left the waterfall behind them, they noticed that the breeze was now less damp. With that the light became dim and they began to encounter patches of bare wall with increasing frequency until G'fand was forced to relight the torch.

Ronin had estimated that they had descended over a kilometer—although they had actually walked many times that—when he spied something ahead. A lighter patch of darkness. Cautiously but with an increasing sense of anticipation, they approached it. And at last they found themselves standing at the end of the tunnel.

Before them a wide ramp led down to a broad avenue that seemed to be roughly the center of a dizzying jumble of buildings extending away on all sides, vanishing in the thick air. The structures were bewildering in their construction, each one a complex of styles and shapes apparently mortared together at random. Large windows crowded upon small ones, balconies cut into rooftops of abutting buildings, what they took to be doorways hung suspended five and six stories above street level.

G'fand gaped. And for an instant Ronin experienced a vertigo so intense that he almost fell. He blinked. And breathed slowly and deeply, exhaling more than he inhaled to empty his system and replenish it.

Beside him, G'fand whispered in an awed voice, "It is. It must be. The City of Ten Thousand Paths." Ronin looked at his transfigured face. "The city of our forefathers, where everything was possible. Ronin, I could have been anything I desired here. They knew —so much, so much." He shook his head and gripped Ronin's arm. "You do not know what this means! It is like a dream—all that I wished for and had no hope of obtaining. It is all here!"

Ronin smiled briefly. "Do you remember when we were young they used to frighten us when we were mischievous with tales of the City of Ten Thousand Paths?"

G'fand could not tear his eyes away from the cityscape. "Yes." He nodded. "They tried to scare me, but I paid them little heed. As a child I was afraid of nothing."

"And now?"

His breath quickened. His voice was a whisper. "And now—now I am frightened of a great many things."

THE sweet smell of ancient decay was in the air, and the soft dry tickle at the back of the throat caused by eons of fine dust floating like gravid spores, cloying, as if they had entered a garden filled with dying flowers.

And they went down the broad ramp into a dense and appalling silence. The creak of their leather, the soft slap of their boots against the rough metal, seemed to be swallowed whole in that vast bowl of quietude.

They tried to use the central avenue but found that, inexplicably, no doorways or windows were to be found on the sides of the buildings facing them. So they were obliged, perforce, to choose at random one of the narrow, twisting streets of which there were a bewildering profusion.

Numerous balconies of all sizes sculpted with decorative cementwork hung above their heads and very little light filtered through the maze of architecture. Yet it was enough to see satisfactorily without the aid of the torch.

* * *

And the city was not without an aura, promising a mysteriousness like the aroma of an exotic spice sniffed from far away: powerful, elusive.

The streets were cobbled in stone, slightly rounded down the center so that it was higher than the sides. They shone dully in the diffused light. There was no sign of refuse or decay out here although sections of the cobbles appeared to be so dark that it seemed as if dirt had been ground into them for centuries until it was now part of the stone.

They heard it at the same time, their heads lifted, questing. It had sounded like the tail end of a growl. They stopped and listened but the silence had closed down upon them again so that even the sounds of their breathing seemed muffled and peculiar to them. They drew their swords, glint of light on polished metal.

Ronin pointed with the tip of his blade to a small wooden door set in a two-story building just behind them. G'fand nodded. They moved carefully along the cobbles, aware that they were not used to the surface. G'fand flattened himself against the wall of the building just beyond the door as Ronin inched it open with the toe of his boot and stood back.

The interior was dark. They heard no sound. Ronin made a sign and G'fand nodded again and they went swiftly and silently through the doorway. Ronin immediately stepped to one side so that his body would not be silhouetted by the light from outside. He turned, and shoved G'fand to the side, into the shadows.

The room appeared to be much larger than he had anticipated because it was very deep. He could make out wooden beams set at intervals along the low ceiling and the deep shadows of heavy furniture. Nothing moved.

Then there came a low cough from a corner and now they could make out two red pinpoints, low, glowing, remote. Outside, the golden light filtered down and the silence hung like a thick winter's shroud. The pinpoints moved and there was another cough, louder, more menacing. The red eyes stared unblinkingly at him, black pupils at their centers very small. They advanced on him. Outside, the silence was a protection against danger, the light spilling like thick honey assuring safe passage. It was part of another world, as remote and unattainable as the Salamander's atrium.

Ronin crouched, turned sideways, gripped his sword with both hands, muscles along his arms and thighs tensing as he heard the soft scraping.

The eyes, half a meter above the floor, were not human, of that he was certain. He moved slowly to the left, attempting to coax the thing into the light from the open doorway, but it kept steadfastly to the darkness. The scraping came again. Ronin was now almost shoulder to shoulder with G'fand.

The thing moved toward them and below the baleful gaze of the eyes a very dim glow of long yellow teeth appeared and then winked out. A soft clicking. The cough came again, and Ronin advanced to meet the shape, moving into the deeper shadows.

"Come back—" G'fand whispered, but he was cut short by a clear dry laugh.

Light blazed in front of them, illuminating the room: a torch.

"Frost!" breathed G'fand.

Ronin looked first at the little man, because he held the torch. He was on a staircase off to their right, which they had not been able to see before. He walked down the wooden stairs and over to the thing, which crouched two meters in front of them, touching a hand to its back. He had an odd gait.

"Ahahaha! Hynd guards the way," said the little man in a peculiar raspy voice. He grinned ingenuously.

He was not over a meter in height, his gaunt face belying his thick, barrel chest. He had long, white hair held in place by a dark leather band and a grizzled beard with more gray than white in it. He had a high forehead and cheekbones, a long, thin nose, dark green eyes set wide apart. Ronin was certain that his skin had a yellowish tinge. His mouth split again as he laughed.

The thing, which he now scratched behind its small ears, and to which Ronin now directed his attention, had a different countenance entirely. It had a long wicked-looking snout covered in short, brown fur and its large, red eyes gleamed from out of a long, tapering skull. Its body was perhaps two meters in length, its four legs ending in clawed toes. It had a long, thin tail that whipped back and forth like a piece of wire. The body was shiny, covered in a hide ridged and scaly. The whiskers on its snout flicked the air continuously. In all, it partially resembled the rodents that inhabited the Freehold's walls. Except for the size.

"Allow me to introduce myself," said the little man. "I am Bonneduce the Last." He bowed, then cocked his head quizzically. "And you are—?".

Ronin told him.

"And of course you have already met Hynd,"

laughed Bonneduce the Last, "my friend and protector."

The animal coughed again, and Ronin saw clearly the sharpness of its teeth. The little man bent to its ear. "Friends." It was like an exhalation. "Friends."

"You take a great deal for granted," G'fand said. Ronin sheathed his sword.

Bonneduce the Last lifted his thick eyebrows. "Is that so? You are from up there." He gestured. "There is no reason for you to wish me harm. Quite the contrary."

"Huh," grunted G'fand. "You have not met with our Security daggam."

"How did you know we were from the Freehold?" asked Ronin softly.

"Bones told me," the little man answered, his head still cocked.

"What?" G'fand sheathed his blade.

"But I have forgotten my manners," said Bonneduce the Last. "You must forgive me setting Hynd out. After all, one cannot be too careful; no indeed, not these days." He sighed, walked to a wall, and set the torch in a blackened metal niche. Ronin saw then that one leg was shorter than the other. "Times past it was different, oh my, yes. One could walk the paths with no need of protection at all." He turned back to them. "But that was a long time ago, a long time"—he shook his head—"before the Dark Sections. But now—" He shrugged resignedly. "Well, times change, bringing with them their own fortunes."

He waved an arm. "But come, make yourselves comfortable, for I know that you have traveled hard and far this day. And please, do not be concerned with

Hynd." He touched the animal on the snout and it lay down with a sigh. "You see, he knows you now—your scent—he will not harm you."

They sat in wide comfortable chairs while Bonneduce the Last closed the front door and went to fetch wine and food.

The dark paneled walls, the tall heavily carved cabinets, the huge stone fireplace filled with fragrant black wood and white ashes, the massive plush chairs in which they reclined, all exuded age and a singular kind of dignity.

Hynd had put his long snout on his forepaws and was now asleep. From somewhere within the depths of the house they heard a soft precise ticking. G'fand rose and moved about the room, peering at objects of unreflective metal and polished stone, running his fingertips along the edges of the sculpted wood. His face was dark and worried.

Ronin looked at him. "What troubles you?"

G'fand tapped distractedly at the wood. "I am ashamed to tell you. I—do not know. You told me what the Magic Man said, about there being people on the surface, people on the planet other than those in the Freehold. You know, to be told all your life that one thing is true, to believe it, even though it is not what you want to believe—oh, this is not making any sense." He turned to Ronin. "But now that we have actually met another being, I—" He glanced quickly at the sleeping animal. "Can we trust him, do you think?"

"Pull up that chair," Ronin said softly. "Now listen carefully to me. This discovery is quite incredible but there are too many ramifications for me to be able to spend any time being shocked. It is true that we know virtually nothing about this man, who he is, where he comes from—although it is certain he is not from here despite the fact that he seems familiar enough with the city. Which is the point. I was sent here to find a manuscript. The Magic Man told me it would be difficult, but Chill take him! he did not explain just *how* difficult it would be. I think he knew precisely how much to tell me in order to keep my interest. This city is so huge that we could spend countless Cycles here and not find the manuscript." He turned his head momentarily to make sure that they were still alone. "Now this can be invaluable to us. I know what to look for, where it resides; perhaps he can tell us how to get there. He—"

They heard a small noise, and the subject of their discussion returned carrying an enormous silver tray with finely etched sides loaded with plates of fired clay, glazed and shiny, wooden bowls of food, and skins of wine.

"I trust that I have brought you enough to eat," he said. "But there is more inside." He set the tray down on a low table in front of them.

While they ate hungrily, the little man talked. He turned to G'fand. "I perceive that you are still somewhat wary of Hynd. I do not want that, so perhaps an explanation is in order. You see"—he patted his short leg as he walked over to a high wooden stool—"I cannot move as swiftly as I once did." He chuckled. "I disagreed with something that tried to eat me." He pulled over the stool and sat near them, his short leg swinging back and forth. "He saved my life—"

"From what?" interrupted G'fand.

The little man's face darkened. "You would not be-
live me if I told you."

"Oh, I would be most in—"

"Do you know what he is?"

"Part rodent," Ronin said.

Bonneduce the Last nodded, obviously pleased.
"Yes, indeed. Quite correct. But as you can see, he is a
hybrid, a cross—"

"—between two different species of animals," finished G'fand.

The little man raised his eyebrows. "Aha, we have a
scholar in our midst," he exclaimed, delighted. "Oh,
yes. Hynd is part crocodile, a water creature which I
believe died out centuries ago. You see before you the
product of millennia of change." He leaned down and
gently stroked the horny back. It rippled slightly and
Hynd made a small sound in his sleep. "Many peoples
believed that crocodiles were gods," he said.

G'fand wiped his hands. "Will you aid us, we have
come in search of—"

"Please." Bonneduce the Last held up his hands.
"Whatever it is will wait now. You are tired. Rest first.
Then we shall talk."

"But we have little time," said G'fand.

Bonneduce the Last slipped down off the stool and
walked in his odd gait to the front door. "One does not
hurry here." He slid a thick bolt across the door.
"Darkness is here. It brings things on its heels, things
you are better off not encountering." He turned and
went to the fireplace. "That is why you met Hynd first.
I knew of your coming but not when you would ar-
rive." He knelt and began to light the fire. "Night was
falling as you came and I take no chances, not these

days anyway. Had you come in my yesterdays you would have encountered me first." The flames shot up all at once and the room glowed with light and warmth. They began to feel drowsy with their stomachs full, the heat beside them, and the tensions of the journey finally dissipating. "But now, we are in a different age, and nightmares stalk the world."

Ronin, at the edge of sleep, came awake. "What do you mean?"

Bonneduce the Last stood up with his back to the fire and stretched. "More anon. Now sleep must come. Blankets are in the cupboard and here is a pitcher of water and a basin. These chairs are large and Hynd is here." He started up the stairs, then stopped and turned. "In the morning we shall talk of your purpose in coming to the City and I shall aid you as best I may." They heard his uneven footsteps climbing the stairs after he was lost to sight.

"What do you think?" G'fand asked as he opened the cupboard and pulled out two woven blankets.

Ronin was splashing water onto his face. He shrugged. "We have little choice. This seems to be a safer place than we could find on our own." He removed his corselet and shirt, pouring water over the shirt in an attempt to get out the dried blood that had seeped through the corselet's mesh. "I cannot see that he means us harm, despite what you may think of the animal. He is right, best to get some sleep. The morning will take care of itself."

Something reached down and pulled him out of sleep. At first he thought it was a sound and he was at once fully awake. The quiet, sonorous ticking, the gentle collapse of ashen logs in the fireplace. Nothing more.

G'fand slept peacefully in the chair across from him. He looked at Hynd. The creature was awake, staring intently at the front door, as if he could see through it. He gave a low cough.

Ronin uncovered himself. The blanket slipped to the floor with barely a rustle. Hynd's ears twitched but he did not turn his head. Ronin grasped the hilt of his sword and stood quietly next to the creature. He strained his ears but could hear nothing outside.

After a time, Hynd's ears twitched twice, then he lowered his head, closed his eyes, and apparently went to sleep. Ronin exhaled a long breath.

His shirt was still wet but he donned his corselet and went back into the recesses of the room. He had it in mind to discover the source of the ticking, but as he passed the foot of the stairs, he heard a tiny sound from above. He paused. Oddly, the sound carried clearly on the heavy air. He turned and silently climbed the stairs.

There were two rooms, roughly the same size, both accessible from a square hallway. Light danced in one room and Ronin went to the doorway, peered in.

Bonneduce the Last knelt on a small rug of intricate and peculiar design with his back to the doorway. "Come in, Ronin, come in," he said without turning.

Ronin knelt beside him. The little man held several small objects in his fist. He shook them lightly.

"Did you hear me on the stairs?" asked Ronin.

"I knew you would hear the sounds." And the white shapes tumbled from his opened palm onto the bare floor. He stared intently at them for long minutes.

There were seven in all. Glyphs were etched into their many sides. He scooped them up, shook them again. Ronin heard the tiny rattle.

"I think something was at the door," Ronin said softly. "Hynd was up."

The little man nodded. "I have no doubt. His hearing is quite keen." He flung the pieces onto the floor once again.

"Those are the Bones," Ronin whispered.

Bonneduce the Last studied them with his green eyes but said nothing until he had gathered them up into his hand.

"The Bones, yes," and his voice was like the tolling of a far-off bell. "I roll the Bones." A sadness came into his eyes, a terrible light shining far back in their recesses, like the agony of ages. "I am aptly named, you see." He rolled the Bones upon the floor and their tiny clatter seemed now to echo with tantalizing intimations. He scooped them up.

"They are so ancient that even I cannot trace their lineage. They are used and passed on. It is said that they are fashioned from the ivory teeth of the giant crocodile, a godlike creature that was purported to have lived in a certain valley, along the banks of a wide rich muddy river." He shrugged. "It is quite possible. Indeed, they are carved of a singular ivory."

Very softly Ronin said, "And what do they tell you, the Bones, when you roll them?"

Bonneduce the Last shook them in his fist and cocked his head to one side. "Why, I should think that would be obvious," he answered. "I see what is to be."

The Bones rattled in his hand. "Of course they cannot tell me everything and frequently the outcomes of those occurrences which interest me most are denied me. Some events are clear, others are merely vague outlines." He shrugged. "But it is what I do."

There was a long silence after he had rolled the Bones once more. And then, for the first time, he spoke while they were upon the floor. "They talk about you," he said slowly.

Ronin felt a moment of irrational chill. "It is nonsense," he said. "I do not wish to hear it."

The little man stared at the pieces of ivory. "You do not fear it," he said simply. "Why then?"

The question had such innocence that Ronin was momentarily taken aback. Then something crawled within him again. "I do not know." His palm strayed to the gleaming hilt of his sword.

"You do not fear death," Bonneduce the Last said, with a peculiar intonation. "That is good, for soon you shall understand its impermanence. Yet deep within you lies a fear which you—"

"Enough!" cried Ronin, lurching to his feet and striking out at the grouping of ivory with his boot. They skittered across the floor. Bonneduce the Last did not move, nor did he speak. He knelt in the same position and did not turn as Ronin angrily strode from the room, even after the sound of his boots could be heard descending the ancient stairs.

Eventually, Bonneduce the Last sighed deeply and got up, made his limping way across the old wooden floorboards. He bent here and there, retrieving the scattered Bones, piece by piece, until he had them all in the palm of his hand. They had never felt so heavy to him, and he gripped them until his knuckles shone as white as the ivory.

He paused then, as if he were to be allowed a choice. He shook his head, and limped slowly back to the rug of intricate and peculiar design, kneeling as before. Very slowly and very deliberately he rolled the Bones upon the floor, and read what their configuration revealed. He wiped the warm ,sweat from his palms by rubbing them down his breeches.

He scooped up the Bones and rather more quickly now rolled them six more times, so that at length he had rolled them a total of seven times. To see if it would make any difference.

It did not. And he shivered involuntarily.

Golden light streamed down, its slanting rays interrupted and diffused by the ornate structures on all sides. The alleyway was narrow and cramped and mysterious as it wended its meandering way through the bewildering labyrinth of the City.

Dust motes danced in the pale light and the silence had a thickness that he now wore with a grateful intensity. He had gone past the sleeping G'fand and, ignoring Hynd's curious stare, had unbolted the door and strode quickly but at random along the alley until he could no longer see the house.

He stopped at last and sat on an old and dusty wooden keg, outside the open doorway to a shop, its time-beaten sign swinging from a black metal pole above his head. The sign was virtually blank now, scrubbed of all but a few scraps of glyphs, mute but unbroken.

He drew one leg up against his chest, letting the

other hang, the heel rapping softly against the side of the keg. It sounded hollow. He closed his eyes and leaned his head back against the small-paned window of the shop. He tried to think of why he had stopped the little man from speaking, but nothing came to him. He thought, At least I should be curious. He was. But—

"Where is he?"

G'fand looked up and dropped the cold bone from last night's meal into the other remnants of the food that had not beel cleared away. He wiped his greasy lips on the back of his sleeve. He shrugged. "I just got up. I thought perhaps he was upstairs."

The little man descended the stairs, saw that the bolt was off the door. "Out then," he said, and set about gathering up the dishes.

"Is it safe?" asked G'fand, getting up. He put his hands at the small of his back and stretched.

"Oh, perfectly. Hynd will see to him."

G'fand frowned. "What does that mean?"

The voice drifted in from the recesses of the house. "I imagine he is out catching breakfast while keeping an eye on our friend."

G'fand walked about the room restlessly until the little man returned carrying a fresh skin of wine. "You seem quite familiar with this city." He made a sharp gesture at the windows with the edge of his hand. He turned. "It is the City of Ten Thousand Paths, as Ronin said."

Bonneduce the Last poured wine for G'fand. "It is," he said without pause.

The Scholar crossed the room, looked out a window. Dust clouded his view. He wiped a small leaded pane with his sleeve but it did little good; the glass, like the cobbles of the streets, seemed ingrained with dirt. "So ancient." It was almost a whisper, as quiet as a tear falling. "Yet you know all about it."

Bonneduce the Last placed the wine skin on the low table before him. "I know many things." Perhaps too many, he thought.

"Then tell me," G'fand said with great bitterness, "how we could evolve from the people who created these wonders."

"You are a scholar, are you not?"

G'fand's eyes blazed briefly but his voice held a note of despair. "Now you mock me."

The little man crossed to him with his peculiar stride. He seemed genuinely grieved. "No, no, lad. You must not think that." He touched G'fand, indicated that he should sit. They went back to the middle of the room and G'fand reached compulsively for the wine. "No, you see, I wanted to be sure."

The Scholar looked up. "Of what?"

"That you really did not know."

"I could have been lying," G'fand said with some indignation.

The little man's face creased as he laughed. "I think not."

Eventually G'fand allowed himself to smile for a moment. "You will tell me then?"

Just a boy, thought Bonneduce the Last. And he said, "Yes." He sat down across from G'fand, the large chair towering over him comically. He crossed his ankles, rubbed his maimed leg along the thigh. "When the time came," he began quietly, "to quit the surface of the world, when there was no other choice but to perish—which many did, by the way—the remnants of the states and nations sent the leading proponents of their cultures to work on the enormous project of carving out a hospitable home beneath the planet's crust."

G'fand was transfixed by the little man's voice, which held tremendous force despite its softness. He was startled when the voice ceased and Bonneduce the Last cocked his head as if listening to a far-off sound. G'fand listened also but all he could hear was the dark and sonorous ticking from the interior of the house.

After a time, the little man continued. "The mages and the men of science—you call them Magic Men, I believe—were forever at war because, I suppose, the foundations of their work are diametrically opposed. At the time of the city's formation, the mages held sway, and so with the unwilling help of the men of science they created the City of Ten Thousand Paths." Bonneduce the Last sighed a little and his extraordinary emerald eyes turned inward momentarily. "It could have been the beginning of dreams; there was room enough for all here. Perhaps they did not work at it, who knows?" He stood abruptly and went to a glass cabinet along the far wall. His hands moved and he returned holding two bits of dull metal. He threw them casually toward G'fand, who caught them instinctively. "Press them together," said the little man. And although the bits seemed identical, G'fand could only keep them together by exerting a great deal of pressure; they naturally pushed each other away.

Bonneduce the Last sat once more and gestured with his head. "Like the metal, the different factions repelled each other. Gradually, the mages began to lose control and the men of science gained ascendancy. In the end, they would have nothing to do with the city their forefathers had helped build under duress, and so they led those that would follow them—a goodly number—upward into the virgin rock above the city because it was fabulously rich in the ores and metals they required, and because it was easier to seal off the city from above. And they constructed the Freehold. And now, over time—" He shrugged expressively.

There was soft silence for a long time, heavy and lusterless, laden with thoughts of fallen history and forgotten faces.

G'fand shivered involuntarily and got up, leaving the bits of metal apart on the table. Several times he appeared about to say something and each time changed his mind. Finally he said in a choked voice, as if it were difficult for him to articulate, "We are told that no one lives on the surface of the world. The elements will not allow it."

The little man, who had been watching him, smiled bleakly. "So. It depends where you are." He went and returned the bits of metal to their case. "The ice reaches farther every day."

G'fand stared at him, his heart racing. "Then it's true. Men do walk the surface."

"Naturally. Did you think I live down here? I must come from time to time—"

"Why did you come this time?"

"To meet some people."

G'fand leaned forward. "Who?"

Bonneduce the Last was silent.

The Scholar gave a tiny exclamation of sound, as if

he had been hit in the stomach, and he relaxed back into the chair. "I do not want to know," he said, his lips barely moving. And he was talking to himself.

Bonneduce the Last was as still as a statue, his eyes lost in shadow beneath his bushy brows.

"What is it like Up there?" The question floated on the air like unused smoke and quite suddenly it was most important that he know.

"Perhaps you will see for yourself soon," said the little man, knowing that it was not enough.

G'fand stood over him and said in anguish, "I must know now."

"This is a desperate time," said Bonneduce the Last. "I have not been to the City of Ten Thousand Paths in a long while. In that time, many things have died and many things have come into being. Evil things." He shook his head.

G'fand knelt before him. "Look, I want some answers. Is that really so much to ask?"

Bonneduce the Last stared at G'fand for a time and there was a sadness in his eyes that the Scholar did not understand. He looked suddenly older. Around them, the ticking sounded like a constant admonition. At length the little man said, "I will tell you what I am able."

G'fand nodded. "What are you doing here then?"

He spread his hands. "I will know that only after it is done."

The Scholar's face twisted. "You make a fool of me."

"Believe me, I do not. It is the truth."

"All right. Suppose I can believe that. I am beginning to see that perhaps anything is possible. Tell me then who you are."

"You do not want to know that."

G'fand's annoyance grew. "I just asked you, did I not?"

The sadness came to Bonneduce the Last's eyes again. "Yes," he said softly. "You have asked."

Ronin's eyes snapped open. He sat very still and inhaled again to make sure of the direction. The sharp smell came from behind him: the interior of the shop. He lowered his leg slowly so that they both were against the side of the keg. He heard movement now, stealthy and difficult to discern.

He drew his sword and leaped to the street, whirling. He heard scufflings, then scratchings and small pantings. He went inside.

It was cool and dark and it took him a moment to adjust and he knew that it was a mistake because anything or anyone smart enough would have attacked him immediately.

Nothing rushed him. There was a heavy snap as of a wooden board being split and then a brief inhuman cry. He moved warily between huge wooden casks. Wine? He pulled cobwebs off his face.

Directly ahead of him he heard a cough. He crouched, sword ready, and saw the red eyes, the long muzzle. The mouth split suddenly, oddly akin to an absurd grin. The long teeth were dark, appeared wet.

Hynd padded up to him and coughed again, softly. Behind the animal, in the darkness, he could just make out the twisted mass of a broken carcass. He put a hand out, tentatively touched the soft fur of the muzzle.

They went out together into the alleyway and the light, and Ronin saw the blood still dripping from the long snout.

"Well," he said, walking alongside the creature, in and out of the bars and patches of shadows, "I trust you have eaten your fill."

For more than a Spell they followed the little lane as it made its crooked way through the city. For a while dark, narrow alleys led off the lane to right and left—often at peculiar angles. Then abruptly, solid walls lined their path, unbroken, windowless, and doorless. Long narrow balconies with fluted scrollwork ran above their heads, so what illumination they had was thin and watery. The walls were of rough stucco, chipped here and there, discolored near the bottom, or unglazed brick with pronounced striations, as if they had been manufactured in layers.

The lane was fairly straight, which only increased their uneasiness. Should they encounter any hostile life—according to Bonneduce the Last, there was an abundance of that—they would have no room to maneuver and only one path of retreat.

However, nothing approached them, and at last they began again to pass wandering side streets. Sometime after this they encountered a fork in the lane.

"Scrolls?" he had said. "There are countless scrolls housed in different sections of the city."

Ronin had reached out the slip of fabric. "Yes, well, perhaps this will help." He gave it to the little man, indicating with a finger the glyphs the Magic Man had written.

Bonneduce the Last had nodded, as if to himself, and Ronin had thought he heard him say, "It is clear now, yes," but he could not be sure.

"I was told," Ronin had said, "that it would be in a private house and not a library."

"Quite so," the little man had said.

"You know the scroll?" G'fand had asked.

"No, no. But I recognize this glyph style. It could only come from Ama-no-mori, an isle I know very little about—I doubt anyone does."

"Then it does not come from here," Ronin had said.

"Well, yes and no. The City of Ten Thousand Paths brought with it, when it went below, emissaries from many lands and many cities. Ama-no-mori, the floating world, sent a great magus, dor-Sefrith, who caused to be built a house of glazed green brick in a certain section of the city. Therein, I believe, you will find the scroll. If you can reach it."

The triangular building directly ahead of them created the fork. Off to the right they could make out a wide street that nevertheless seemed quite cluttered with what looked to be collapsed building materials. Dusty light dappled the ancient cobbles and, perhaps because of the haze, the shadows seemed to shift and waver. To the left tall, arabesqued buildings cast deep shadows into the street for as far as they could see.

As they moved into the mottled shadows of the street on their left, Ronin recalled what the little man had said: "I shall describe your route but I must warn you that it takes you through a Dark Section. It cannot

be avoided if you are to make the journey and return
by nightfall. You *must* return by nightfall, is that clear?
Too many things abroad at night, too many. Stay to the
path I give you and do not falter. Remember, speed is
of the essence because the city keeps changing now. I
trust this will get you through."

The cobbled street was cool and they shivered a little. Stone creatures, grotesque and fantastic of visage,
leered down at them from cornices and buttresses.

"How I wish there was more time," lamented
G'fand, his eyes moving over the architecture, drink-
ing it in. "There is so much to learn here."

"You know we cannot tarry."

"Yes." He nodded sadly. "Bonneduce the Last is
right. There is so much danger now."

Ronin glanced at him, on the point of asking him
what had changed his mind about the little man, when
the faint susurration reached his ears. One moment
the silence seeped sluggishly along the walls of the high
buildings, muffling the creaking of their leather, the
soft chink of metal on metal from their gear, the next
they seemed to be surrounded by sound. It was as if
they were hearing, through some trick of architectural
acoustics, the combined voices of a multitude. The
murmuring as it came upon them, like waves upon a
lone and desolate shore, words blurred and indistinct,
held overtones, a presence, a superreality.

They looked in all directions but could make out
nothing in the gloom. There was no doorway close to
them, no window; the narrow balconies were empty.

"What is it?" G'fand asked.

Ronin said, "We are in a Dark Section." His hand
strayed to the hilt of his sword.

They moved on, and still the stone carvings regarded them, lips pulled back from bared teeth, and the sea of sound licked along the humped length of the crooked street, increasing in volume.

There was no space between buildings here, although they obviously were separated by walls on the inside, for they passed numerous doors now with individual, excessively carved fronts that seemed somehow unsteady, as if about to give way and expose the bare skeletons of the structures. As they advanced, an increasing number of windows opened onto the street. There appeared to be no order in their placement. They crowded one another in profusion, some just centimeters apart, others overlapping in chaotic riot.

Often, at the periphery of their vision, the pair thought they could detect movement behind the windows, furtive and unnatural, but each time their eyes darted to the spot, it was gone. G'fand particularly seemed disturbed by this.

The muttering continued unabated from all about them, which, unaccountably, increased the sensation they had of being watched. It occurred to Ronin then that there was a cadence to the sounds and, beyond a rhythm, melody.

They rushed on, almost at a trot, the jangle of metal against metal all but drowned in the pulsing sound. Chanting, Ronin thought. He told G'fand, who listened through his mounting unease, and nodded. But, he said, it was nothing he had ever read about. The words, long meaningless syllables, nevertheless chilled them. And as if one were the cause of the other, the shadows deepened and a cold wind blew along the street.

The chanting was louder now, swelling like an engulfing tide, and Ronin increased their pace until they were running headlong down the lane. The Bladesman in him abhorred this flight; his training was for Combat and his immediate reaction was to turn and find the source of the chanting, which seemed somehow to be affecting their senses.

They were running slowly, too slowly, the dark windows crawling by, the air so gluey and sticking to them that they had to cleave a path through it. And all the while the sound advanced on them from behind, rolling over them heavily.

But through the murk Ronin realized that Combat now was time-consuming and useless. At the back of his brain a tiny voice screamed and screamed: Get out! The trouble was that it was getting softer, and he had to strain to hear it, to remember what it was screaming.

Once or twice G'fand paused, panting, moving toward the houses, and Ronin, not quite knowing why, pulled him back, set him to running again.

But it was hard, the cobbles slippery and suddenly insubstantial, the breath pounding in their lungs. Small chitterings assailed them, and heavy slitherings from behind them, gruntings and weird moanings, so that the backs of their necks crawled. Tears seemed to be streaming from G'fand's eyes. The street closed in upon them and the stone creatures above their heads proliferated, flocking on the overhanging ledges.

And still they ran, with a dogged singlemindedness now. Shrieks came from behind them, closer now, and the chanting, ritualistic, almost liturgical, reached its peak. Stone walls turned to rubber.

Both of them saw the light of the cross street at the same time, Ronin blinking his eyes to keep the connection so that his pumping legs would know where to go. G'fand began to waver, slowing down, and Ronin reached out blindly, dragging him forward toward the light. Why? he thought. Waves of sound washed over him and his vision went momentarily. Then someone, from very far away, a distant bright land, said: "Get out!" And his legs dragged themselves forward, one last lunge, the screaming came—what?—ignore, forward to the slitherings, light and . . .

They stood in what appeared to be a wide avenue. Light streamed into their eyes, dusty and golden. G'fand dropped to the cobbles, chest heaving. Ronin turned, peering back into the deep shadows of the narrow lane. Nothing emerged, and—his head lifted— yes, sweet silence descended onto his aching ears.

Old shops lined either side of the avenue, their doorways open, small-paned windows dusty and dim. Above, their signs, of scarred wood and beaten brass, creaked in the warm breeze. Higher still, where one might expect windows to be, were solid walls of fired brick and mortar, broken at regular intervals by deftly carved stonework.

"They are not decorative."

"What?"

The Scholar pointed. "The carvings on these buildings. Those are glyphs, very old, but still—"

"Messages?"

"Their history, perhaps. If I only had time—"

The avenue described a turning to the left and they followed this at a fast pace and abruptly found themselves at the edge of a vast plaza. The warm light shone unhindered here and G'fand scanned the vault above them in an attempt to discover the source. Near them now were only low buildings, but in the distance tall structures rose, their outlines blurred in the haze.

As they walked out into the plaza they noted that it was floored with alternating segments of deep brown and light tan stone, the former laced with chips of a mineral that caught the light and threw it back at them in dazzling pinpoints. The stones were precisely cut in shapes roughly like a triangle with its top point cut off so that it formed a four-sided figure, wider at one end. They were larger along the perimeter of the plaza and grew gradually smaller as the pair progressed toward the center.

They came upon several low wide benches of a textured sandy stone, polished along the seat, grouped in a semicircle around a low oval structure. They sat gratefully down and rested for a time in the heavy molten light.

Ronin took a long pull from the waterpipe and ate some food without really tasting it. G'fand went to inspect the oval in front of them. It was perhaps a meter in height, lidless and hollow. G'fand stooped, found a small piece of rubble, dropped it down. After a long time there came a faint splash.

Ronin got up and joined him.

"A well," said G'fand. "But judging by the water level, it has not been of much use lately."

The walls of the well, constructed from the same sandy stone as the benches, were covered by the same style of carving as they had seen on the avenue. G'fand sat on his haunches to get a better look.

"Can you make anything of it?"

G'fand frowned in concentration. "Uhm, well, it is quite a sophisticated language—more than our own." He pointed with a forefinger. "You see here, judging by the relatively infrequent repetitions, the glyph range must be enormous." He shook his head sadly. "Give me, oh, twelve or fourteen Sign and the right texts—although I suppose I could make do without—given more time, and I might be able to read this. Now—" But he was still excited and would not leave the side of the well until Ronin, deciding that it was time to move on, spoke to him.

He looked up then, reluctantly, and seemed about to say something, when a movement caught his eye and he motioned to Ronin.

Off in the distance, three or four animallike shapes moved among another grouping of benches. At first Ronin thought that they would move in another direction, but then the breeze freshened and he knew that they were downwind, and if the animals had not noticed them by now, they soon would.

The animals came out from under the benches, started hesitantly toward them. There were five of them; four-legged, long muzzles, dingy yellow fur, matted and dirty. They crept closer, and now he could make them out clearly: long forelimbs, hind legs short and thick with bunched muscles, so that they appeared to be crouching as they moved. Squat necks merged into wide, powerful-looking shoulders. Their snouts were all mouth.

As they approached from the far side of the well, they spread in a rough semicircle. G'fand stood. He could see their eyes now; hot, lemon circles with tiny, black pupils.

Ronin slipped his sword from its scabbard. "Take the right side."

At the same instant, they stepped from behind the cover of the well.

Black lips drew back from blood-red gums to reveal long curving fangs, blackened, wet with saliva, set in triple rows. The animal nearest Ronin yawned nervously, its jaws hinging open to an impossible angle. Its mouth snapped shut with a clash, and it licked its lips. The eyes regarded him feverishly.

He moved out to his left, reaching for his dagger, flicking it before him with his left hand, facing the animal with his side.

It blurred before his eyes and he knew it was leaping, but it was coming on his left flank instead of straight on. Impossible! He made a pass with the dagger but too late, and the blur was past him and, simultaneously, a second animal bounded at him from in front. The mistake was in treating them as dumb animals, and as the first one had gone beyond him he had corrected his thinking so that now, at the instant of the dual assault from front and rear, he had his legs far apart, knees bent to help absorb impact, the sideways stance already an enormous advantage because the left hand slashed upward with the dagger while the right arced the double-edged sword. The long blade clove the first animal's skull in twain, spraying bits of yellow brain and shards of bone. Almost at the same time, the second animal was upon him, larger and more massive than the other. He tried vainly to flick it from him but the combination of mass and momentum was too much, and it landed upon his left shoulder, spit on the dagger, howling and shuddering as a great gout of black blood splattered hotly against him, viscous and sticky, the stench of it clinging to his nostrils so that for a moment he had trouble breathing. Staggering under the assault, he tried to avoid the long sinewy forepaws reaching for his eyes, scythelike claws scraping the air, great jaws snapping, eyes rolling. Jerking his left hand, raking the dagger through the thing's insides, knowing his right arm was useless as long as the animal was on him, and still it writhed desperately against him. Then something smashed into his side and all the breath went out of him. Flesh came off in strips and he crashed to the stone tiles of the plaza.

On the right of the well, G'fand faced two animals. Nervousness and exhilaration combined within him. Both hands on his sword hilt, he feinted to his right, swung to the left, catching a beast in mid-spring, opening its chest and deflecting somewhat its body. At the same time, he did his best to keep out of the second animal's way.

Ronin had reflexively let go of the dagger. Still he sprawled in the black blood and slime of the dying animal. Pain raced along his side and dimly he wondered how the blow had gotten through the mail corselet. He turned onto his back and saw the beast—the third one—poised to smite him again with its powerful forepaw. He struggled to get up as the animal crouched low, recognized there was no time, and channeled all his energy into a mighty two-handed cut. He did not have the leverage that he would have had on his feet, but it was timing and swinging sword and arms as one, using the pivot of his wide shoulders as the power base. The beast leaped at him, so close that he felt the warm puff of fetid breath as the enormous jaws swung wide, heard the thin whine of the talons ripping the air before his head. He swung from right to left, the blade whistling for an instant before it struck the hide, bit into flesh, and Ronin leaned his torso to the right, using the added leverage as the blade cracked the beast's spine and the carcass danced lazily, black blood pumping in spurts, fluttering in the air like funereal lace. The animal toppled in a twisted heap to the paving.

G'fand could not concentrate on both so he ignored the wounded one, attacking the second beast. He knew it was a mistake when he felt the weight of the first one crash onto his back. He staggered, went to his knees, his vision a blur. Then, miraculously, the thing was off him and he felt lighter than air, springing up and slicing into the neck of the advancing second animal with his bloody blade, oblivious to the impact of its forepaw against his shoulder, swinging again and again even after the creature ceased to twitch.

After a time he was dimly aware of a hand on his shoulder, and he turned, staggering slightly to see Ronin standing over the animal he had wounded and forgotten about, the one that had almost killed him. He saw then that Ronin was grinning and he knew that even through his tiredness, his spent exhilaration, he was returning it.

They wiped their wet weapons on the matted pelts and, leaving the corpses where they had fallen, went across the vast plaza, reluctant in the end to leave it, to plunge back into the midst of narrow streets, dark and confined: the recesses of this enigmatic city.

They worked their way down a crooked alleyway,

turned right, then right again. They were in a section of the city containing low rambling houses with some space between them. As a result, this area was divided fairly evenly into square blocks. It was lighter here, though not as light as in the plaza, and for once the streets appeared to run quite straight.

They saw small animals, some looking much like the rodents of the Freehold, others bearing no resemblance to any creature they had encountered before. But all seemed small and likely presented little threat to them.

Occasionally they spotted large slitted eyes peering out at them from a dark doorway or a back alley, but there seemed to be no aggressiveness in the stares, only fright. G'fand commented on this, his spirits high, but Ronin was unaccountably worried by what lurked in those eyes. He tried to shake off the feeling, reasoning that they were now quite near the house of glazed brick. Yet it continued to grow.

Ahead lay the last few turnings. It was deathly still. The small skitterings and occasional chatter of the animals had ceased. In the abrupt absence of sound, he fancied he heard the chanting from the Dark Section. But there was nothing on the air.

They moved around a corner and, at last, caught sight of the house of glazed brick, its canted copper roof glowing in the late light. For a long moment they drank in the sight. G'fand gave a short cheer and Ronin smiled. Then they went down the street, Ronin leading the way.

Ronin, intent on his goal, had just passed a doorway, oversized and gaping blankly, when he simultaneously smelled a sickly wet stench and felt a wave of coldness at the back of his neck.

He drew his blade, spun, its tip catching the light, saw G'fand slammed against the doorframe as he was whipped into the interior of the building. A muffled scream brought him up short as he hurtled through the doorway.

G'fand had not even had time to withdraw his sword. His arms were pinioned at his side. A huge shape gripped him, its dimensions ill defined. Ronin rushed the shape. He had a flashing glimpse of hooded orange eyes, a protrusion, black and strange underneath, and then his sword swung into the thing.

He grimaced as needles of fire raced up his arms like vibrations. His fingers went numb and only by pulling with his free hand on the hilt was he able to disengage the blade. Immediately, the pain subsided.

He panted, wiping the sweat from his eyes, peered into the gloom. The hulk took on some form. It was at least three meters high, with muscled truncated legs terminating in some form of clawed paw or hoof. The light was too dim for Ronin to be sure. A thick and sinous tail whipped from the rear of the body. The thing's outline kept changing, pulsing like a heartbeat. Then its head swiveled and he saw its face. His breath was a sharp hiss through clenched teeth. His skin crawled.

It had long slitted eyes with narrow inhuman vertical pupils that pulsed with the creature's outline. Two irregular gashes in the flesh served as nostrils. Underneath yawned a mottled, hideous beak, wickedly curved and honed, a stunted, rigid tongue throbbing grotesquely.

G'fand still struggled feebly in its terrible embrace. Ronin lunged, slashing with the sword. It sank into the scaly flesh and again he gasped as the agony raced through him. He pulled free, swung again and again. And sound came from that frightful maw, a swift ululation, and he knew that it had not been harmed by his attack. G'fand was limp now within the thing's grasp, and cold sweat broke out on Ronin's face as, heedless of the paralysis weakening his arms, he attacked once again.

Alien, orange eyes blasting out of the darkness, and the air became thick with the fetid stench of the thing, clotting in Ronin's throat so that his stomach heaved and his lungs labored as he put all his strength into the arcing blade that clove the air again and again, ceaselessly, and he was a machine now, a machine of death and destruction, the adrenaline pumping through his veins holding against the pain. He ground his teeth, his muscles jumped as he pushed them to their limits. And still the creature stood before him, the shell of its beak working.

His vision began to blur and he was dimly aware that his reflexes had become slowed. Something thick and heavy was moving toward him; he felt the hot wind of its approach, but the connections refused to work and he could not move away, and it whipped into him, rough and scaly, along the side of his head, and his body was thrown violently forward. He fought desperately for balance, lost, reeled into a wall. Just before unconsciousness came, he thought the creature looked toward the recesses of the interior, then he dropped down an endless stairwell into pitch-black-ness.

How beautiful it looked, so far above him. Freed by the distance, floating warm and safe. Watching the pale amber light striking obliquely so far away, his de-tachment was complete. The stippled patterns wavered in the uncertain light. How nice to be lying here at the bottom of the well, watching the world through the distant oval window, dreamily, drifting. He thought idly of rising up and climbing toward the smoky bright-ness, but he felt too tired. Alone, adrift.

And then he blinked and it broke apart like a bub-ble rising through water to the surface. He stared blankly at the circle of amber light thrown against the ceiling. He blinked again and full awareness swept over him.

He tried to sit up. Too fast. Made it halfway before his head pulsed with pain. He edged himself along the floor until he put his back against a wall. He sat like that with his head in his hands, relaxing his muscles through force of will, allowing the ache to flow out of them.

He looked for G'fand, found him stretched out on the floor two meters away, deathly pale. Dragging the body slowly over it felt like two kilometers. Feeling faint breath still within the chest, he unstrapped the waterpipe and fed G'fand water so that he choked a little and the lungs began working more fully. Only then did Ronin gulp thirstily at the pipe. He felt imme-diately refreshed and went to retrieve his sword.

When he returned, G'fand was sitting up. He

rubbed his palms across his face. "Frost, I feel like I've been crushed," he whispered. "Is that thing gone?"

Ronin helped him to his feet. "Yes. Are you dizzy?"

G'fand waved away his support. "No. No." He walked slightly stiff-legged to the doorway, leaned against it. "The end of our journey. After all this, I trust that the scroll we seek lies within."

The house of green-glazed brick beckoned in lazy quietude. It stood at the end of the street, a cul-de-sac, and it was unusual enough in this city of unusual architecture to command the entire area. For one thing, it appeared to be many-sided. For another, the sides sloped inward as they rose, so that the second story was smaller than the first. The glossy bricks were of singular construction: they showed no age; the house looked as if it might have been built last Cycle for all the wear visible.

There were no windows on the sides that faced them. A giant wooden door banded in thick iron strips dominated the front side of the house. Broad steps of black stone with pink and gold veins running through it, polished to a high sheen, led up to the door, which, they saw now that they were close to it, was in fact a slab of red copper. Perhaps a trick of the oblique light had caused it to take on the appearance of wood.

A ring of black iron, twisting in an endless circle, formed the handle of the door. Ronin grasped it firmly and, putting his shoulder against the copper slab, pushed inward.

There came a soft, dry click, as distinct and close as the sound of an insect in a field of high grass on a quiet summer's day, and the door opened.

The odor of spices greeted them, pungent and ingrained in the air as if someone had lit a fragrant fire of aromatic leaves and green twigs and kept it burning for many Sign.

They were in a long high hallway, the ceiling an arch above them, the floor a narrow path of dark, polished wood planks laid straight down the center. Open spaces, deep and dark, between the floor and the walls on either side, gave them the feeling of being suspended in space.

The hallway terminated in three doors of a peculiar polished wood with deep-red grain, banded in beaten brass. Glyphs were carved into each door. Ronin turned to G'fand. "Can you make anything of these?"

G'fand studied each door. "I lack the knowledge to be sure. But—" He peered again at the glyphs. "Try the third one."

Turning the burnished brass handle, Ronin found that it opened easily enough.

The first level consisted of six rooms. Thin, exquisitely woven rugs covered the floors, small dark wooden cabinets stood against the walls, which were hung with tapestries of singular manufacture depicting the hunting of strange and grotesque creatures, the paying of tribute to ornately costumed men and women who appeared to be some kind of Saardin. Upon the carpets were numerous low tables of glass and brass within which resided myriad small treasures of cut jewels, ivory, and faience. There was no sign of age, not even a trace of dust.

Within the fourth room, Ronin found an ornate stairway to the second story. G'fand was busily moving from glass table to glass table, plainly fascinated by the artifacts. Ronin looked about him. "Make certain you have seen everything down here," he called to G'fand. "Then come upstairs and join me." So saying, he ascended the stairs.

There were three rooms. One was obviously a sleeping chamber, and one, Ronin surmised, an alchemical chamber of some sort, judging by the equipment. The last room was the one he was searching for. Books lined two walls from floor to ceiling—he saw with some surprise that the room was hexagonal. Another wall contained only a six-sided mirror of beaten and polished silver rimmed in deep-green, black-veined onyx, lustrous, translucent. The adjacent wall was filled with racks of scrolls, some rolled on polished wooden dowels, and he crossed to them at once, searching for the glyph heading the Magic Man had written down.

A quicksilver flash caught the periphery of his vision. He turned his head. It seemed to have come from the mirror, but when he looked around he could find nothing in the room that was likely to cause a reflection.

He went over to the mirror and stared at his face. And the flash came again, like light on moving water, dazzling him momentarily.

He no longer stares at himself, but at a formlessness of light and color, absorbing and infinite. Motion. Hurtling through the patterns, forward, headlong. He experiences a slight sensation of vertigo, the exhilaration of flying, and he hears a soft rustle, as of a forest of leaves blown on a quickening wind.

Abruptly he is in a cool place made all of richly veined marble, lit warmly but dimly. And vast, for he hears the echoes: perhaps voices, the quiet slap of sandals, the rustle of fabric against flesh, tones of discord and harmony.

From a height he drifts through columnated hallways and high-vaulted chambers and gradually he becomes aware of the molten throb of unfamiliar instruments, pounding skins, trip-rolled and muffled, lazy dark chords under gyring melody, hears the peregrine music unfurling, haunting, electric.

A great night-black bird swoops down upon him, wide wings beating the liquid air, and he tries to cover his face, a reflexive motion, and discovers he has no body. He floats, insubstantial, an essence. And still the bird, long feathers shining, stares at him with unblinking crimson and black eyes. Its talons are enormous. Gripped within one is a writhing lizard. The talons open and the creature drops into a fire burning far below. The bird opens its long beak and human laughter booms out.

He sees K'reen then. Her back is to him as she talks to a dark figure which towers over her, but he recognizes the soft bell of her hair, a forest of texture, the shape of her body, silken of skin, hard of muscle, the orbits of her gestures. The figure screams silently at her, slaps her across the face, again and again. Her head whips from side to side. She turns suddenly and looks up at him, and he starts in shock. She has his face, tearful and saddened.

He is in another place within the marble building. Or perhaps it is another building all of marble. A long hallway. Far away at the other end is a tall figure clothed in black lacquered armor ribbed and banded in sea-green jade and twilight-blue lapis lazuli. Perhaps he wears a helm, for his head is oddly shaped, at once chilling and familiar, although he is too distant and the light is too uncertain to say why. Two swords of unequal length hang from his sides in scabbards so long that they almost touch the marble floor. His hands glitter as the figure looks about as if searching for something. Then he strides from the hallway.

Something cold comes. The incense braziers shudder on their bronze chains. A wind is rising. He feels a presence, very close. A frigid wisp, a seeking tendril— *of what?*—writhes and touches his mind. He recoils, as if seared by a blade burning like ice. Below, in the hallway of eternal marble, frigid fires begin to rage, pale and insatiable. He cannot breathe. He gasps and chokes on the dread creeping into him, washing away all resolve. He feels weak and powerless, a child storm-tossed and alone.

Abruptly, within the chaos of his being, through the terror and desperation, he feels sparks of water against his face and body, and he lifts his head to the roiling of purple clouds. And electric clashing is in his ears, and the surface upon which he stands trembles. White light rings the opening sky. He reaches for the pale hand.

The flash comes again, like light on moving water, dazzling him momentarily.

"—not downstairs," said G'fand from directly behind him.

He started.

"Say, what are you doing? The scrolls are over here."

Ronin blinked, licked his dry lips. "I thought—I saw something in the mirror," he said thickly.

G'fand stepped closer. "What mirror?"

Ronin focused and saw a six-sided plate of iron,

perfectly plain and unreflective. The onyx border seemed to wink at him in the light. He shook his head. The house of a magus.

Then he shrugged and turned. "Come," he said.

They took them systematically, by rows. Once, as he worked, he glanced at the six-sided thing on the wall. And thought of what he had experienced, of what it meant. He was certain, now, that Borros spoke the truth: there was a habitable world on the surface. But why the Salamander should choose to lie to him, he had no idea. However, it was clear to him that he was amid a drama of enormous proportions. He understood its nature not at all, yet he would be a fool to ignore the hints at its scope. Up until now boredom and curiosity and a curious perversity, which he always recognized in himself yet was like quicksilver, his strength, and, he imagined, perhaps his ultimate downfall, had guided him to this strange place. Why else was he here? He gave a mental shrug and got on with the search.

The scroll was not there. It seemed inconceivable to them that they could have come so far, overcome all that they had, for naught. Returning empty-handed was not an eventuality Ronin had spent any time considering. To him it was not a matter of the value of the scroll.

He sent G'fand to search the other rooms on this story while he looked around here. The floor was bare, the dark wood planks rubbed to a high gloss. Again no dust or wear was evident. Over by the walls of books were a pair of low stools unlike any he had seen before. They were constructed of buffed leather, stiff but worn beneath the polish. They were convex, two sides sloping down, the narrower ends curving up, and were attached to crossed wooden legs by a heavy leather strap with an adjustable brass buckle.

Along the wall most closely opposite the door, several glass cases gleamed dully in the light. He crossed to them, saw there were three. The first was empty, although two indentations on the green felt of the bottom indicated that at one time two objects about the size of a large man's hand had lain there. The second case contained an oversized book, from all appearances quite old, opened midway through. A blue fabric marker ran down one page. Both pages were blank. Ronin moved to the third case, where he saw what seemed to be a replica of a hallway, roofless so that one could easily view the interior. It appeared to be constructed of marble. Twelve columns lined the hallway, tiny metal braziers hung at intervals. The model was extraordinarily detailed, the workmanship superb. Ronin leaned closer and the shock of recognition hit him at once. This was a replica of the hallway in the mirror that was not a mirror! He glanced over his shoulder at its blind face once again.

He turned back to the miniature. Here was where the armored warrior had stood, and there was the entrance through which the terrible presence had been about to enter. He heard again in his mind the lure of the music. He lifted the glass top. As soon as he did so something caught his eye. A sliver of light yellow from under the marble floor. He stared at it for a moment until it struck him what it must be.

He drew his dagger and slipped the point under the side of the replica, lifting slowly, but it did not give. He tried along one end, and was able, after moments of experimentation, to pry it up.

With mounting excitement, he drew out the sheet, knowing somehow that at the top would be written the line of glyphs for which they had been searching. The miniature fell back into place as he released it, and he called to G'fand, as he stared at the black line of their inscription. Below, the scroll was covered from top to bottom with close-written glyphs.

They clapped each other on the back. G'fand held it as they descended the wide curving staircase. He shook his head. "It is a language I cannot even begin to understand."

Ronin took it from him. "Someone will have to decipher it." He rolled it into as tight a cylinder as he was able. "Now that we have it, I shall make sure that we do not lose it."

The shadows were long, the slanting light deep amber as they went down the black stone steps, the gold veins iridescent. The city seemed peaceful; the dense quiet acquiring a languorous luster as the day waned. They set off back the way they had come, tired but jubilant at the success of their quest.

Perhaps it was the sounds of their voices or the buoyancy of their mood or the vista of the jumbled city, somehow more familiar, that lay before them bathed in the warm light.

Or perhaps it was something else altogether that caused him to fail to see the movement behind them. It came swiftly. A sharp cloying odor. He whirled and his sword was out in the same motion. But it was too late. He was slammed as if by a giant's fist and he reeled into the gutter, tumbling upon the cobbles. Crimson fire was in his lungs and all the breath went out of him. He tried to inhale, gasped weakly.

Through a haze he saw the creature that had attacked them just before they reached the magus's house. Its thick sinuous tail lashed back and forth continuously as it reached curved talons toward G'fand. He had drawn his sword and was doing his best to defend himself. It was ineffectual.

Ronin tried to rise but it was as if he were paralyzed. He lay in the gutter, striving to raise his sword, struggling to breathe, watching the thing close with G'fand. The hideous beak opened and closed spasmodically, and then it took hold of G'fand's sword along the blade. The metal crumbled within the grip of its six-fingered hands.

With a mighty effort Ronin came up on his knees, leaning on his sword, head shaking like that of a wounded animal. He gained his feet, staggered, searched for balance. His sword clanged onto the cobbles. Drawing his dagger, he ran at the creature from behind.

Its talons were at G'fand's throat, squeezing. He looked helpless and stunned. Ronin smelled the awful stench and the coldness just before he slammed into the thing's back. It was like hitting a wall. It ignored him. He climbed upon its back, saw dimly G'fand's legs dangling in the air, his eyes bulging. Then the pain engulfed him. Bolts of fire penetrated his flesh and he fought back a scream. Time shifted.

He was a microbe upon a mountain, climbing hopelessly. The dagger in his hand writhed uncontrollably and he almost let it go, but the sight of G'fand's twisted, pain-filled face was before him, and it drove him on. The pain moved through his body and his lower half began to go numb. His legs and feet still churned for purchase on the scaly hide but he could not feel them, they were parts of someone else's body. Still he clawed upward with his free hand and dagger-filled fist. He gasped at the stinking air, but his lungs would not hold the foulness, and he retched, eyes watering. He concentrated on the shining point of the short blade.

All strength seemed to flow out of him. The numbness began to creep upward. Soon it would be at his brain and he knew he would be finished. Far away in another world he heard a terrible sound, horribly malformed, as if a human voice were being forced through an alien larynx. Far away in another world his body was freezing. Far away into another world he was slipping—

Desperately he forced his eyes open, stared into an infinity of orange coldness, black irises like shards of obsidian, as large as planets. Laughter.

He drew upon his last resources of will, and with a supreme effort, with his final surge of strength, he forced the blade through the air. Pale hand slipping into his at the center of his being. And he ripped it point first into the gaping maw.

Renewed foulness smote him and he retched violently. Dimly he was aware of a thin screaming like the unbearable tension of a singing wire. He rammed it in with all his power, twisting the blade mightily. Brought both hands onto the hilt.

Abruptly there came a sharp snap, a vibration, and an enormous convulsion, and the howling reached a peak. With that he sank down into a velvet blackness against which he at first tried to struggle, and then from which he was too tired even to return.

He awoke all at once with the terrible stench of the thing still in his nostrils. He coughed, wiped his mouth. All around him the cobbles were shining and slippery with streaks of crimson and viscous pools of black. There was no sign of the creature but G'fand lay several meters from him. He got up slowly and carefully, went over, knelt beside him. G'fand's eyes bulged and his tongue protruded thickly from his blue lips. There was pink foam on his chin, drying now. His skin held a faint luminescence. His neck was canted at an unnatural angle. His throat had been rent into ribbons of red cartilage.

Ronin's colorless eyes were opaque as he reached out and gently closed the Scholar's eyes. He sat on his haunches amid the offal of the battle and stared at G'fand. Many thoughts ran through his mind but they were as confused and unreachable as a school of darting fish in deep water.

The shadows lengthened slowly, wheeling about the ancient enigmatic buildings, staining the aged cobbles. Far off an animal barked, a short, sharp, startling sound, and close by, small creatures, perhaps attracted by the scent of fresh blood, could be heard, tiny claws skittering along an alleyway.

To all these sounds Ronin was oblivious. He stared, his breathing labored, at a torn and bloody corpse that had once thought and talked and felt joy and sorrow.

* * *

He got up. The ache of his muscles seemed very distant. He bent and gently picked up G'fand's body, eased it over his shoulder. It felt as light as a feather. He went across the glittering cobbles to get his sword. The toe of his boot kicked something that went clattering over the street. The hilt of his dagger, shorn of its blade. He sheathed his sword.

In the plaza the glint of the tiles was dull in the fading light. He found the corpses of the animals they had killed already half eaten. He looked around, but nothing moved over the broad expanse.

He went to the well and, without pausing for a moment, dropped G'fand's body down the shaft. After a long time, he heard the splash and it seemed to him no louder than the sound the piece of rubble had made.

Darkness was falling, its thick shawl snuffing the last of the long amber shafts of light, the encroaching shadows now dominating the streets, when at last he stood before the scarred door of Bonneduce the Last, and leaned his weary body against the warm wood. He could not remember how he had gotten there. He heard a snuffling from behind him, near, in the lane. It sounded somehow familiar, as if it had accompanied him for a while, but he was too exhausted to turn his head and look.

Through the door he heard Hynd's low cough, and then it was thrown open and he collapsed at the feet of Bonneduce the Last.

Bonneduce the Last had already been on his way down the stairs when he heard Hynd's cough. In one hand he held an old leather double shoulder bag. He put something into it and said, "Almost time." Then he threw the bag across a chair, crossed the room with remarkable alacrity, his shoulder dipping with each stride of his short leg. He pulled open the front door.

Hynd rushed out into the lane, growling, jaws working. He bit into something, tore away a tremendous chunk of flesh. Bonneduce the Last heard the yelp of pain as he dragged Ronin across the room and settled him into one of the large soft chairs. Hynd trotted in, licking his lips, and used his long muzzle to close the door. Then he lay down and watched the little man minister to Ronin.

By the time he had spent some minutes stripping off Ronin's corselet, the metal blackened and ripped, and removed the tattered remains of his shirt, his eyes had gone cold and hard. The lines on his face seemed to be more pronounced.

"Already the Makkon are abroad," he said. "Even here they have come."

Hynd's head came up, and now he stood at the door, a silent sentinel. The little man pulled his leather bag to him, drew out a packet of ointment, which he applied to Ronin's chest and arms. He spoke to Hynd. "The Bones can tell me only so much. The young one I knew would not come back." His hands worked swiftly and surely. "I am past feeling for them, the Bones have seen to that, else I would have gone mad. It is what I must do."

Bonneduce the Last went into the interior of the house, returned with a goblet of water. Into this he dropped several grains of a coarse brown powder, which he fed to Ronin as best he could. As much ran down his chin as went into his mouth.

"He will sleep now as his body recovers." He threw the remains of the liquid into the cold ashes of the fireplace. "He has suffered much, now. And he will suffer more. Yet it has to be. Out of pain he must be forged."

He got up then, went briefly again into the interior. When he came back he held a small object of brown onyx and red jade. He slipped it into his bag. "And now, one thing yet remains to be done before we quit this city." He reached something out from his leather bag, held it for a moment, feeling its texture with his fingertips. "Yes," he said softly, "it becomes clearer, piece by piece." He placed the object on the table beside the sleeping Ronin.

He awoke to silence, deep and complete. But it was somehow hollow and empty and he spent some time attempting to determine why. He knew precisely where he was. Then he had it: the ticking was gone.

With that he rose and called out. No one answered. He went across the room and quickly up the stairs, aware that most of the pain had gone from his body. The rooms were bare. It was the same downstairs. No signs remained that either Bonneduce the Last or Hynd had ever been there.

He sat down again in the chair. Morning light was streaming in through the dusty grimed windows, bright and fresh and new. Idly he traced the beams of light, slanting in, and his eyes came to rest on a gauntlet spangled by the light, lying on top of the table next to the chair; the only foreign object in the house.

He picked it up and immediately he was struck by its singularity. It was heavy and there appeared to be no seams except along each fingertip, almost as if the closing of the apertures had been made by shearing off nails. Then two bits of information came to him at once: the scaly texture of the gauntlet and the fact that it had six fingers. It cannot be, he thought with a shock. But the longer he examined it the more convinced he became. He was holding a gauntlet made from the hand of the creature he and G'fand had fought; the thing that had killed the Scholar. Something blazed far back in his eyes. He recalled the trek to the plaza, the small splash of the body, knew that at that precise moment an irrevocable step had been taken. And he had done it.

Without further thought, he pulled on the gauntlet with his left hand, flexing his fingers. The light turned the scales to silver, reflective and brilliant.

He left the house then, and strode down the crooked lane, the air cool and fresh against his face, to start his return to Borros and the Freehold far above him.

THEY were glittery. Wet-looking yet opaque. They were an entire universe, seeing everything now; seeing nothing. What struck him most deeply, however, were the lines of fear etched into the features. And the red marks. Must it come in such a manner? He was becoming an expert on it: Death.

He stood in the lamplight of the Medicine Man's side room. He had come there to see Borros and had not found him.

He stared down at the body on the bed. The heavy, lined face so frightened in life. The rheumy eyes were glazed. He thought, What have they done to you, Stahlig?

The flame from the sole lamp flickered in the draught. The door to the Corridor opened and Ronin's hand went instinctively to the hilt of his sword.

"I truly wish you would try it," said Freidal softly. Ronin turned slowly, saw the Security Saardin and three daggam. Freidal went over to the concealed door, opened it. Four more daggam stepped through.

His mouth curled in the parody of a smile. "Come, come. Where are the heroics that a Bladesman should be famous for?" His voice was silken with subdued triumph. "Will you not fight your way out? Take us all on?" His good eye stared with intensity. "Take his weapons," he barked, and they disarmed him. Freidal had chosen the place well, he thought. No room to maneuver in such a small area. No chance.

Freidal's face was a mask. His slick hair glistened. He looked relaxed, almost happy. "Did you believe for a moment that you could drop from our Levels without my knowledge?" The ghost of a smile played along his thin, white lips. "Stupid boy!" His tongue clucked reprovingly against the roof of his mouth. "You were warned. A courtesy which you chose to ignore." Freidal stepped closer to him, and daggam on either side gripped Ronin's wrists, although he had made no movement.

The Saardin reached out and removed Ronin's corselet, stared at the welts along his chest. "As I knew you would." He ran a finger across the bruised flesh. "You see, I could not get what I wanted from the accursed Magic Man. The fool! But it was purely accidental." He laughed, a sharp, disquieting sound. "I knew it would work then, throwing you and Borros together."

His finger was at Ronin's waist. "Ah, and what is this?" He grasped Ronin's right arm and the daggam on that side let go. He brought the forearm and hand up. The gauntlet shot silver through the tiny room. Freidal pulled it off Ronin's hand, examining it. "Could this be it? What he sent you Downshaft to find?" He looked up, into Ronin's face, said sharply,

"Is it?" The false eye flashed. "It has begun, you know, the struggle for power."

Ronin thought of Nirren. Where was he now? He had not been able to locate him before he had left, and now this weighed heavily upon him, as if he had violated a trust. But, he told himself, I had no idea it would begin so soon. Could my knowledge of Borros's project have helped him? There was no way to tell now.

Freidal grasped his elbow and swung him around. "He did not die well. He tried to protect you but his fear won out. He helped." Ronin recalled his agitation, his warning. The old man had tried to tell him. "How does that make you feel? And you see what he is now. A piece of meat, stinking and putrefying." His nostrils dilated and he sniffed delicately. "Dead things offend me. But Stahlig was put here for a reason. Even a stupid boy like you can see that." He jerked Ronin around and motioned to two daggam, who removed the corpse. Freidal fondled the scaled gauntlet. "Be sensible. If you have no interest in power, at least look after your life." He stroked Ronin's chest with a cold palm. "It would be a great pity to destroy this body." He slapped the gauntlet against the side of his leg. "Can the Machine work?"

Abruptly there was a commotion outside in the dark surgery. Freidal started, as if he had forgotten that beyond these walls, the intimacies of the moment, existed the world of the Freehold. He turned his head, as did Ronin.

They saw that three men in close-fitting breeches and jerkins of a soft tan color had pushed past the daggam who had just returned from disposing of the body. The man in front was slim, with red cheeks and full lips. The jewel-hilted daggers glittered over his heart and at his hip.

"Saardin," he said blandly.

"Voss," Freidal acknowledged coldly. "What is the meaning of this intrusion?"

Voss saw Ronin. "Ah, there you are! We have all been quite concerned about you." He smiled winningly. "None the worse for your interview with Security, I trust!"

Freidal's good eye flicked in its socket and a muscle spasmed in his cheek. "This behavior is inexcusable! Bakka! Turis! See these people out immediately!"

The Chondrin held up his hand. "One moment, Saardin. The Salamander wishes to see Ronin. He has been distressed over his whereabouts. His safety, you know—"

Two spots of color burned on Freidal's cheeks. "What are you saying?" He was trembling with suppressed rage. "Have you taken leave of your senses? This is strictly a Security matter."

Voss smiled icily. "No. I am afraid you are mistaken."

The good eye blazed at the Chondrin, then Freidal turned abruptly, making a cutting gesture through the air with the edge of one hand. "Take him then," he said thickly. "Take him and get out!"

Voss motioned to one of his men, who took Ronin's weapons from the daggam. Then he stepped up to Freidal and said, "He will want this too." He slipped the gauntlet from the Saardin's hand, and the four of them departed.

* * *

The woman with the broad face was gone. A Bladesman sat in her place. They went through the inner double doors and down the hallway. At the end, the Bladesman carrying Ronin's weapons handed them to Voss and he and his fellow disappeared through the door on the right.

Voss opened the opposite door and led Ronin into a low-ceilinged room lit by lamps. There were no Overheads. The walls were dark and bare. Across the room was another door. There was a single wooden chair in the center of the room. Voss indicated that Ronin should sit. Ronin shrugged. He had no illusions as to why he was here. He had been witness to too many events; and too many people were gone.

The sharp smell of cloves foretold the approach. He had not heard a door open. The Salamander stood over Ronin. He wore black shirt and breeches and gleaming thigh-length boots. A fine mesh vest of red gold winked in the light. He wore a wide crimson leather belt from which a scabbarded sword hung. The ruby lizard was at his throat.

Voss, leaning on Ronin's sword, handed the Salamander the gauntlet. The big man grunted, turning the thing over in his large hands. "So?"

Voss shrugged. "Apparently he brought it from Downshaft."

The Salamander stared at Ronin. "How far did you go?"

"All the way."

He glanced at Voss. "No wonder Freidal was interested."

Ronin heard a tiny sound behind him, as if someone had slipped into the room, but the Salamander did not turn and he could not twist in the chair. Perhaps it was nothing.

"My dear boy, I hope you appreciate the great service I have done you. Freidal can be most unpleasant when he has a mind to."

Ronin stared into the eyes like black coals. "So I noticed. He killed the Medicine Man."

"Oh?" The Salamander's eyebrows raised. "What a pity. You knew him a long time." He spread his hands. "I am most sorry."

"The Magic Man too, I imagine."

"Oh, dear me, no. He could hardly afford to do that. No, Borros is much too valuable. He is being detained several Levels below us."

"I was not aware that you knew so much about him."

"Oh, I see." The Salamander frowned. "That was careless of me." Then he shrugged. "But one hopes, my dear boy, that you can be treated as a friend, an ally—"

"You are as desperate as he is—"

"Not at all, dear boy, not at all. I merely think that you should be back where you belong. There has always been room for you here."

Voss moved minutely, and Ronin said, "To be your Chondrin? You already have one. In any event, we have been through this before. What if I should turn you down a second time?"

The Salamander's expression changed. His eyes smoldered and he smote Ronin across the face. "What an abysmal fool you are. I offered you everything and you spit at me. Did you believe that I could forget?"

"At the time I believed that you would understand—"

"Oh, I understood! I trained you to be the greatest fighting machine in the Freehold. I saw the ability lurking within you. It took a master to bring it out, nurture it, let it blossom. An Instructor could never have accomplished it."

"You make it seem as if it was all your doing."

"But it was! You were there and I molded you. You became what I wished you to become."

"Not quite."

The Salamander bristled, and his voice was as smooth as silk. "I trained you to be my Chondrin; an unbeatable warrior. Did you think that I was wasting my time in picking boys and training them? A reason behind it all. And what was your response? You return the care lavished upon you with insult."

"There was no—"

"Silence!" the Salamander roared. His face was colored by rage. His enormous bulk loomed over Ronin, the threat of death. "Do not presume," he said quietly, icily, "to tell me what I already know." He bent forward and Ronin felt Voss very close at his side and slightly behind him, out of his peripheral vision. "I should have seen it; you lacked the initiative. It all came so easily to you, you never regarded the mental processes as important. That was a mistake; a fatal mistake." The stygian eyes were glittery and fever-bright as they stared at Ronin. "Now Voss has initiative. He—eliminated two other Students of mine in order to ensure his position as Chondrin." He laughed, a short strange sound. "I would not trade him for you. What conceit!" He stood up and looked past Ronin's head for a moment before his eyes returned. "Now we shall see how long it takes for you to tell me what I want to know." He signaled to Voss. "Bring the—"

At that moment the door to the hallway was thrown open and a Bladesman came hurriedly in. The Salamander looked up.

"The Magic Man," the Bladesman said, "has escaped from Security."

The Salamander's eyes flicked again behind Ronin, and he heard a slight movement. "Oh, that fool!" He looked at Voss and threw him the gauntlet. "You know what to do." He whirled and followed the man from the room.

"On your feet," Voss said coldly. He tucked the gauntlet into his leather belt.

He got up and they went out the way they had come in. Six men were in the outer room, two guarding the double doors to the Corridor, and Ronin thought, In that Freidal told the truth: it has begun.

They went out through the doors and Voss prodded him to the right, down the Corridor. He heard a distant clamor, the pounding of boots, the clang of metal, intermittent shouts. He felt the tip of Voss's dagger at his back.

"Where are we headed?" Ronin asked.

"You do not expect an answer to that."

Ronin shrugged.

"How could you have done it?"

Ronin turned his neck, felt the bite of the iron tip. "What?"

"Gone away from him."

"I am what I am."

"Huh! He is right, you *are* a fool! Did you not realize that you were bound to him?"

Ronin said nothing.

"You had a moral obligation—"

And he almost missed it. The silver of shadow along
the wall ahead of them, around the arc of the Corridor, so that he did not think the Voss had seen it. He
kept his pace steady, and thought, Any diversion must
be used; he is most vulnerable here in the Corridor.
Once we get to a destination, there will be little
chance. He thought then of the whirring in the air,
angry and hot, cutting through the sounds of the birds,
the accuracy of Voss's throws.

A man was in front of them, and Voss still had not
seen the small slice of shadow. He must be pressed
against the wall, Ronin thought.

"You owe him your life," Voss said. "Including your
loyalty."

The figure came out from the wall and Ronin
dropped, rolling to the right, across the Corridor,
came up with right arm extended to ward off the expected dagger blow. But Voss was not even looking in
his direction. He stood facing the figure, his face regis-
tering shock.

And Ronin felt the adrenaline pumping. Nirren!
Nirren stood before Voss, bright sword unsheathed,
held before him.

Voss unfroze. "What are you doing so far Upshaft?"

Nirren grinned, his mouth a tight line. "Where were
you taking Ronin?"

"That is no business of yours. Out of the way!"

"And if he chooses not to accompany you?"

"The choice is not his to make."

"I say it is."

Voss's hands became a blur and simultaneously Nirren lunged like a dancer, extending his front leg very low. The sword shot out as the air hummed. Voss's face held a measure of surprise. His eyes were still looking at the jewel-hilted dagger lodged head-high in the far wall as the blade pierced his chest. He stood that way for a moment, his blood running hotly along Nirren's blade. Then his right hand twitched once and, as Nirren withdrew the sword, he crumpled over as if he were made of fabric.

Nirren touched the face with the toe of his boot, the head turned slackly. He swung to face Ronin and grinned. "It is too bad. I would have enjoyed seeing you take him." He shrugged. "Well, where have you been? And G'fand's gone missing."

Ronin went across the Corridor, took his weapons from Voss's corpse. He pulled the gauntlet free from the other's belt. "I have been on a journey Downshaft, for the Magic Man—"

"Then you got through to him!"

"Yes, and I have much to tell you," Ronin said, strapping on his scabbard. They moved toward a nearby Stairwell. "But first I must find the Magic Man. He has escaped from Freidal."

Nirren nodded. "All right. I am in the midst of following that Rodent. At last I believe I know who it is, fantastic though it may seem—"

Ronin cut him off. "Listen, fantastic is the word for what I have learned. The Magic Man is correct; we are not alone on this planet—"

"What?"

They both caught the flash at once, but the thing was already in the air. Nirren's jaws swung wide and he threw his hands up in a vain reflexive motion. A gout of blood erupted along his neck. He staggered back and fell clumsily to the floor.

Ronin raced into the Stairwell but the commotion of running feet and raised voices echoing in the Stairwell made it impossible to tell which way the assailant had fled.

He ran back into the Corridor and knelt beside Nirren. The front of his jerkin was soaked in blood. He ripped off a length of the Chondrin's shirt, withdrew the dagger at his neck, his fingers cold on the jeweled hilt. He put the fabric against the wound. White cloth stained red.

Nirren's eyes were still clear and bright with intelligence. Ronin expected him to ask about the Magic Man's project. Instead he said, "What happened to G'fand? You know."

There was pain in Ronin's eyes. "I took him with me. I thought he would be of help with his knowledge of the glyphs."

"And was he?" The breathing was labored as the body struggled with the shock.

"Yes." Ronin looked into his eyes. "He was killed. He—"

Nirren's body trembled. The cloth at his neck was entirely crimson now. He gripped Ronin's arms and a sadness that Ronin could not understand danced behind his eyes. "The Rodent," he managed to get out with difficulty. "I am sure now, the dagger, go Upshaft, after—" His head fell and Ronin held it. "Last time, follow Up—" He tried to laugh then, choked instead. The light in his eyes was fading; they were opaque, like stones. "Just thinking—team—what a team." His eyes closed as if from fatigue. "All gone now—Ronin, I am sorry." Then the blood, which he had been holding back with a last effort, came out of his mouth.

Three

THE BLADESMEN

UP and up and up. The darkness rushing by and the clamor from below fading, but it was as if a strong wind rushed in his ears and he heard Nirren sighing again, *All gone now,* and knew it was true. The world had collapsed and he was adrift in the dark, directionless. But his legs did not understand. They pumped strongly, up the Stairwell. *Follow Upward,* Nirren had asked, and he would do it now, and he felt the burning within him, the hate growing and pulsing, fed from the secret fires of many events. Surely it was the Rodent who had slain Nirren, for he had been on his trail and had been very close. Closer than he knew. His lungs worked as he raced through the Levels of the Freehold. Upward, ever upward. Once he stared down at his hands, saw with some surprise that he had slipped on the silvered gauntlet and that he clutched the dagger that had killed the Chondrin. Jewels on the hilt? And then Borros came into his mind. Escaped and gone where? Upshaft surely.

He climbed the stairs as far as they would take him.

He emerged into a bright Corridor painted a brilliant yellow. Dust lay thickly along the floor, clung to the walls. He looked down. Bootprints in the dust, confused, but certainly more than one pair.

He sprinted down the Corridor and gradually the color of the walls deepened. There were no doors. On he ran, the hate a living thing within him now. Existence narrowed.

And the Corridor ended. Here near the summit of the Freehold, the Corridor did not describe a complete circle. He faced the black bulge of a Lift's doors. He stabbed at the black sphere and the doors yawned. He stepped inside. Up, ever up. There was one sphere and he pressed it. He ascended. Eyes like stones. *Ronin, I am sorry*, he said. What had he meant? I am the one who is sorry, Nirren. But death comes and there is no way to stop—

The Lift sighed to a halt and the doors opened. Above him the surface of the planet, so near. Perhaps just steps away? He went into the room before him. It was an ellipse, painted red. In the center was a black platform from which a metal ladder ran vertically into a round section cut out of the ceiling. Low doors in the solid platform were open, and he saw what looked like neat piles of clothing. One stack had been tipped over. And the thought grew in his mind. Borros—

A tiny whistle in the air, like a tickle at his ear. He drew his sword and spun. The dagger was in his belt. A sword drove into his, scraping down the length of the blade, smashed into the hilt. Slight, deceptive twisting of his wrist and disengagement was accomplished.

He looked at his opponent and a shock ran through

him. Blood pounded in his temples and for a split second the scene before him seemed to blur.

She stood before him, in leggings and jerkin of a soft tan color. Across her chest ran a thin leather strap to which was attached a red leather scabbard that hung between her breasts.

She stood before him in the oblique combat position, legs apart, knees bent, leading with her shoulder to present a narrower target. Her pale hands gripped a sword the same length as Ronin's. The black torrent of her hair was held back from her face by a plain gold band. It had the appearance of a helm.

She stood before him, small beads of sweat glinting at her hairline. Her eyes were unnaturally bright, the pupils contracted so that they seemed to be all iris. She smiled and it was like the coming of the frost. Her white teeth gleamed, small and even. She looked quite deadly.

"K'reen," he breathed.

She laughed sharply, a bitter sound. "How I have waited to see you at this moment!" she said in a tight voice. She swung at him and he parried solely by instinct. He felt as if the floor had suddenly become molten. He was sinking into it. He could not move. He could not take his eyes from her. She circled him, and they moved out onto the floor, like slow dancers moving to metaled music. She struck again and he parried.

"A Bladesman," he said softly. "Can it be?"

"Come," she said thickly. "Come and find out." She slashed again and again at him, drawing him out, and her eyes flashed coldly, triumphantly as he moved toward her.

He stared at her and realization suddenly flooded

him. Because now she was not beautiful or pretty or any of the other words he would normally associate with her. She was naked to him now, stripped of the layers of femininity. She was at once more and less than she once was, pared and honed and transformed.

She was elemental.

Metal rang against metal in the small oval.

"Here is what I really am!" she said savagely. "Not what you made me out to be. The Salamander saw the potential in me—to be a Bladesman. He was not afraid to reject Tradition. Years we worked in secret, lest the other Saardin suspect and forbid it."

They moved around the oval, she advancing, he retreating. She struck at him continuously, testing, probing.

"Why?" asked Ronin. "Why did he train you?"

She smiled coldly. "Part of the gathering of power." Then she sneered. "Something you would know nothing about."

But it was not right, somehow, and he heard the Salamander saying, *A reason behind it all.* But there was no time; she swept it away. "You could have been his Chondrin!" she hissed, striking at him. "You would have been with him when I came. He would have put us together, and then we could have had everything!"

There was an odd sensation inside him, and he looked at the feral glow in her eyes, the sweat running down her cheeks, her heaving breasts. And he saw what he had not wanted to see before: the jewel-hilted dagger between her breasts. And his gaze moved, as if of its own accord, to her flank, to the scabbard hanging empty there.

"It was you," he whispered. "The Rodent. You killed Nirren. Why? He was our friend."

She shook her head. "The enemy," she said deliberately. "He was the enemy. Just as you are now the enemy—"

"But this makes no sense—"

"You turned your back on him. After he taught you and trained you, you would not serve him. You would not aid him now."

Still he retreated under her blows. "I serve no one," he said softly. "It is the only fact of which I am certain." Then, as if suddenly realizing what she had said: "You were in the room, behind me!"

"Yes!" she hissed. "Ready to embrace you, if you joined us." She swung at him. "He gave you a chance to amend your insult. You mocked him instead."

Where was the woman he had known? Whence had she fled? Could she have felt any fondness toward him? But the emotions he knew, when they had been there, had been genuine. He recognized the fault within himself. Surely he could have seen this side of her, had he only looked. But he had turned from her too many times, and this, he knew, as much as her training, as much as the purpose set for her by the Salamander, was the cause of this confrontation.

"But Nirren—"

"He delayed me," she cut in. "I had not expected him to be so close." He wiped the sweat from his forehead, stood his ground. Sparks flew from the meeting of their weapons. "The delay cost me," she said bitterly. "The old man was faster than I had imagined. I missed him by seconds."

"You mean Borros is on the surface?"

"What is that to you? He will be dead soon enough, frozen and buried under the snow."

But part of him exulted and he knew now what he must do. He shook his head. "You are wrong. He will live. And I will follow him." And he thought, But she is Nirren's killer. In friendship he asked for revenge. *I serve no one.* Sweat rolled along his neck, and he felt a chill. *Ronin, I am sorry.*

She snarled and her teeth looked like those of a small predatory animal. "Oh, no," she said. "This is your tomb." And she lunged at him, arching her blade with all her might, catching him off guard with the unexpectedly powerful blow, and he realized at once that he had underestimated her cunning. They locked blades, and he twisted again, moving his wrist. But she countered and the blades ground together at a peculiar angle. Her sword snapped abruptly, the released force causing his weapon to jump away. She reached between her breasts, withdrew the jewel-hilted dagger. His palm closed over the hilt of the sister blade and he held it before him. This is what she wants, he realized. She is most proficient with the smaller weapon.

They circled each other in the confined space, judging distances and the switch to lighter blades. He wished his head were clearer, but conflicting emotions darted like lightning in his mind, squirting too fast to catch.

Perhaps she saw a hint of this confusion in his eyes, and perhaps that is why she threw herself against him unexpectedly. They tumbled to the floor, locked together, hand clutching wrist, rolling over and over.

Her hot, panting breath was against his face and he smelled her scent as their legs twined and their bodies heaved. They grunted and clung to each other, desperately fighting for position. He stared into her eyes. They were large and deep and liquid and he felt a stirring inside. He thought of what she had done, of what she wanted, and knew the hate was there. He fought to push down the edge of the other emotion. Her enigmatic eyes stared at him and he could not tell whether there was hate or hunger there.

Her heat and her sweat melted into him. Her long hair whipped his face. Her flesh was both hard and soft as it writhed against him. "I'll kill you," she hissed. "I'll kill you." Her thigh was between his legs, imprisoned. She moved it against him and her other leg came over his hip and her calf pressed his buttocks. Desire rose in him like a great feathered bird gaining the air currents. Her voice was low and thick as she said it again, "I want to kill you." But it was almost a moan. Their bodies ground together. He was aware of the press of her breasts against his chest.

Something slammed into the back of his head and a red film clouded his vision as pain laced through him. He had fetched up hard against the platform at the center of the oval. Dazed, he still clung tenaciously to her wrist, but using all her strength she wrenched it away from him and the honed blade of the dagger seemed to pulse in the light.

She was panting through her open mouth, the lips pulled back from the pearl teeth, and her thighs gripped him convulsively as she rocked hard against him. He wanted to lie back and embrace her. He shook his head but it would not clear. She began to shudder. "Kill you," she choked. "Kill you." And with an effort she stopped her eyes from closing. She gripped the dagger, knuckles as white as bone, and she moaned a little as she drove the blade point first toward his throat. Her pelvis ground against him in waves and he looked up to see that her eyes were wet. He saw dimly the terrible flash of light along the moving blade and wondered that he still felt the power of her groin moving against his. He felt suffocated by a great heat and instinctively he put up his hand. As Nirren did; vainly, he thought.

The point of the blade caught his palm. It was his gauntleted hand. The honed tip hit the scales, skidded off harmlessly. Within, his hand never even felt the force of the blow. He shook his head again, and grasped the obliquely moving blade, trying desperately to hold it. But she had both hands on the hilt now and she had the leverage and he had none and she began to force the gleaming point back at him. The cutting edge creased his throat, broke the skin. Blood welled up. But his left hand was free now and it scrabbled along the floor at his side until he found the hilt of the dagger he had dropped. And it was all reflexive now, no thought involved at all. He brought it up very quickly between their bodies, the blade quivering at his throat now, and buried it hilt-deep in her stomach.

Her eyes opened so wide that the whites showed all around the edges, and she grunted thickly, a brief guttural noise that seemed somehow terrible to him. Blood pounded against the back of his eyes and he jerked powerfully on the hilt so that it sliced up between her breasts.

Her head dropped abruptly, as if she had been hit on the back of the neck, and her lips came down over his, warm and soft.

He felt a great, hot pool of wetness between them and convulsively he threw her off him and, panting, swayed to his feet.

She lay on her back, eyes still very wide and shiny, with the jeweled hilt protruding obscenely from between her breasts, sending shards of harsh light reflecting in the blood that covered her.

What have I done? he thought, as he stared at her. *All gone now.* It reverberated in his mind. Waves of blackness seemed to reach up, ready to engulf him, but he fought them off. He staggered across the oval to his sword, sheathed it. Then he went back to the platform, reached into one of the open doors. He let the fabric unfurl. It was silvery, slightly iridescent, and it was very light. It was a close-fitting suit of some sort. He believed he knew its purpose. Quickly now he stripped off his tattered clothes and donned the suit. As he had suspected, it fit him snugly and was very warm. It must retain all the body heat, he thought. Pockets along the sides bulged with concealed packets. Food. He strapped on his weapons belt.

He heard a sound and whirled, blade ready. The doors of the Lift hissed open and a whiff of cloves came to him. He tensed. Something moved within the shadows of the Lift and the immense jet figure of the Salamander stood half illumined in the doorway. His hooded eyes scanned the scene before him.

"Come to stop me yourself?" Ronin snarled, flicking the tip of his blade.

The Salamander smiled with the corners of his mouth, almost contentedly. He did not step into the room. "Oh, no," he said silkily. "Others were to have done that. I see that they have been unsuccessful."

Ronin came forward. "I am leaving," he said slowly and deliberately. "You have lost. You have neither the Magic Man nor the information I possess. Go fight your battle alone."

The Salamander sighed theatrically. "You have become a real menace, dear boy, and must be dealt with. But you still have much to learn." And now he smiled once again. He was delighted with himself. "You have lost quite as much, in your own way, as I. Perhaps more."

Ronin stared at him, blinking back the sweat that rolled down his face, and cursed silently. He inched closer. I'll get you yet, he thought. And said thickly, "Yes, I know."

From deep within the shadows of the Lift, cloaked in his mantle of jet and crimson, the carved ruby lizard a blood splash duskily visible at his throat, the Salamander laughed long and deep. Then he said, "Oh, no, dear boy, you do not know. Yet." His arm extended briefly. "Look at the face at your feet. What do you see? The woman you slept with—"

"And you trained." He was closer now.

"Yes, quite. But all for a purpose." His eyes were dark and unreadable. "We were close, you and`I. Until you—but why bring up old hates?" The Salamander seemed oblivious to Ronin's movement. "My men found her on the Middle Levels. They had heard rumors, you see, of a child found by the Workers. She was regarded as special, they believed that she sprang from the Freehold itself. They told me of this, not a Sign after you had left. And it occurred to me who she might be. But I dared not believe it. It was too improbable, too wonderful a coincidence. I sent them to fetch her and when I saw her I knew. It had to be, for she was no Worker's child. And her age was right. In secrecy I found her and in secrecy I trained her." His voice was thick with triumph now and Ronin shivered in spite of himself. "And then I sent her out. And she was good, very good. She did precisely as I had instructed her. And now she has fulfilled her purpose." He laughed again. "Of course she never knew. Never even suspected. And that made it more delicious!" He was gloating now.

Ronin frowned. "What are you saying?"

"I may not have Borros, or his knowledge. But you," he said delightedly. "You, in obtaining your freedom from this place—you have slain your long-lost and beloved sister." His laughter boomed again, echoing in the oval, as if it had been pent up for centuries.

He tried to reject it but the vision in the Magus's mirror swam up through his mind, and he saw again K'reen turn around to stare at him, turn around with his face. And then small things, minute things, fell into place with the clanging of great metal doors.

He screamed wordlessly and lunged at the Salamander, but his blade scraped along the closed doors and faintly he heard, "Not now, not now." And echoes of the laughter came again.

In a frenzy, he pried at the closed doors with blade and fingers until his nails were torn and bloody, but they would not open. And the time for descent had passed.

After a while he turned and eventually he was able to gaze again upon K'reen's face. Something wailed inside him and he sank to his knees beside her. He touched her face. Can you ever forgive me? he thought. Will I ever be able to forgive myself?

Gently, he closed the eyes. Carefully he stepped over the body and commenced to climb the vertical metal ladder that led to the Access Hatch. The entryway, so many centuries unused, to the surface of the planet. He did not look back.

And had anyone been in the oval to see him, they would not have recognized his face.

ABOUT THE AUTHOR

Eric V. Lustbader has written nine major best sellers and has been praised as "the author of authentic and engrossing oriental intrigue second to none" *Los Angeles Times*. He lives in New York City and in Southhampton, Long Island, with his wife, editor Victoria Schochet Lustbader.